SEASONS
OF THE TRAIL

by Lynn Glaze

Illustrated by Matthew Archambault

SILVER MOON PRESS
NEW YORK

First Silver Moon Press Edition 2000
Copyright © 2000 by Lynn Glaze
Illustrations copyright © 2000 by Matthew Archambault
Edited by Erica Jeffrey

The publisher would like to thank Barbara Magerl, Karen Buck,
and Tom Hunt of the Oregon-California Trails Association
for historical fact checking.

For information:
Silver Moon Press
New York, NY
(800) 874–3320

Library of Congress Cataloging-in-Publication Data

Glaze, Lynn.
   Seasons of the trail / by Lynn Glaze ; illustrated by Matthew Archambault.-- 1st Silver
Moon Press ed.
      p. cm -- (Adventures in America)
   Includes bibliographical references.
   Summary: In 1860, traveling by wagon train from Missouri to California,
fourteen-year-old Lucy finds the discomfort and danger made tolerable by the presence
of two handsome twin brothers.
   ISBN 1-893110-20-6
   [1. Overland journeys to the Pacific--Fiction. 2. Frontier and pioneer life--West
(U.S.)--Fiction. 3. West (U.S.)--Fiction.] I. Archambault, Matthew, ill. II. Title. III.
Series.

PZ7.G4814375 Se 2000
[Fic]--dc21
                                                                              00-030769

10 9 8 7 6 5 4 3 2 1
Printed in the USA

For my great-grandmother, whose story this is,
and for all my family, past and present.

— LG

ONE

LUCY SCOTT PULLED THE HEAVY FARM house door shut and turned to take a last look at the house where she had lived all fourteen years of her life. A damp April breeze ruffled her dark curly hair and flapped the sunbonnet, hanging down her back. She couldn't believe they were actually leaving. The farmhouse was empty now. Her parents had sold most of the family's furniture for money to cover the journey ahead. All they had now was the wagon, stuffed with food, and the few heirlooms—the family Bible, Grandfather's portrait, Grandmother's china, and Mrs. Scott's rocking chair—that her father had said it was all right to take. The rest of her family was down on the road in the covered wagon waiting for her, but she didn't join them yet. She wanted to take it all in: this Missouri farmhouse, the big red barn, the elm trees she had climbed when she was small, the fertile farmland that stretched dewy in the early morning light. The sun was coming up over the fields her father had left fallow, stretching new shadows on the side of the barn.

"Hurry up, Lucy!" Mr. Scott shouted from the road. "We best get started." Lucy turned reluctantly and hurried down the path past budding daffodils,

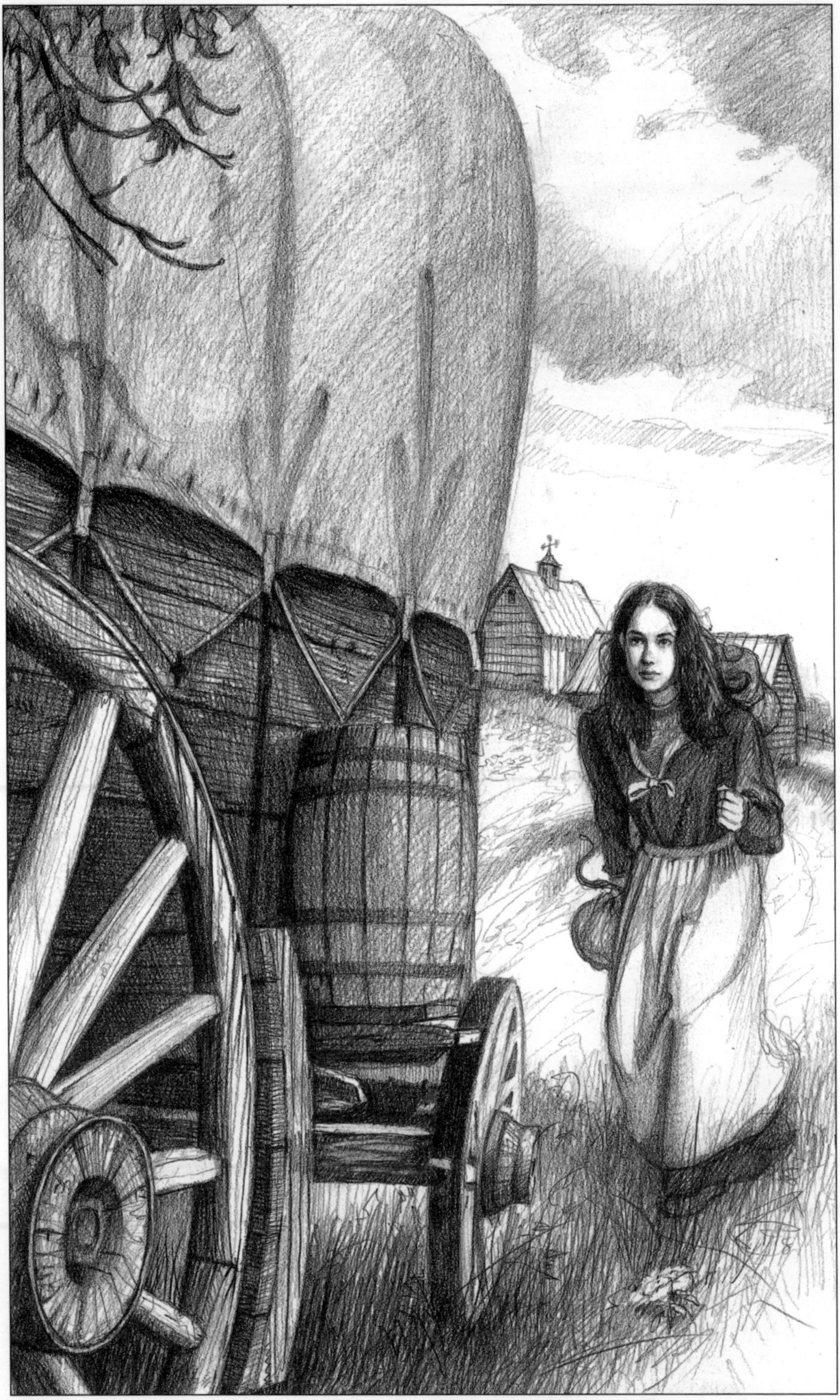

2

toward the narrow wooden wagon with large wheels and a ribbed canopy covered with canvas. Wooden barrels and boxes were strapped on its sides, filled with provisions and tools for the months ahead. Throwing her carpetbag through the opening in the back of the tall wagon, she hitched up her long blue calico dress and hoisted herself up.

Lucy tried to find a place to sit in the heavily loaded wagon without bumping her head on the pots and pans, which hung from the frame overhead. A hair mattress lay on the wagon floor, piled with quilts and pillows. The rest of the wagon was crowded with so many boxes, barrels, and pieces of equipment that there was not one bare spot left. She settled herself on a bag of horse feed and leaned against the portrait of her grandfather that was wrapped in a quilt and wedged against the sideboard.

Julia, her six-year-old sister, sat on the round tub of salt, absent-mindedly chewing on one of her long brown braids. She looked small and pale, squeezed between the barrels of sugar and flour. Julia hadn't said much about going to California, but Lucy didn't think she was very happy about it. Frank, her ten-year-old brother, on the other hand, couldn't be more excited. He sat on a box of dried beans, his red head peeking out the front of the wagon, ready to take in every mile of the journey.

"Here we go!" Mr. Scott's voice boomed from the wagon seat, flicking his whip over the back of their two horses. "California or bust!" Lucy peered out of the back of the wagon at their home, disappearing in clouds of dust kicked up by the wagon wheels.

Frank grinned. "Yeehaa!" he shouted. Lucy gave him a sour look.

It was so early in the morning that their wagon was the only one on the road. They passed tidy farms with white clapboard houses and big red barns like the one they had just left. A neighbor out plowing his fields stopped his plow horses. "Hullo, Mr. Scott. Off already?"

"Yes, the journey to California is a long one. If we don't leave now, we risk crossing the mountains in winter."

The farmer shook his head. "I don't understand why you want to leave this good farmland, but good luck anyway."

"Thanks, we'll need it," Lucy's father said, snapping the whip on the horses' backs again. They plodded north, toward Independence, where they would meet up with other pioneers. Dandelion, the milk cow, tied on behind the wagon, mooed.

They traveled for hours. Lucy's legs cramped from sitting. She felt queasy from the motion of the wagon. Frank and Julia slept sitting up against the sideboards. Lucy wished she could sleep so easily. "When are we going to stop, Father?"

Mr. Scott didn't say anything. Mrs. Scott turned back, her face weary. "Why don't you try writing in the journal I gave you?" she suggested.

"Nothing has happened yet," Lucy protested.

"Maybe it will pass the time," her mother said sharply. Lucy knew she had better not argue.

She sighed and pulled a pencil out of the pocket of her pinafore. Opening the new composition book to the first page, she wrote:

"Lucy Scott's Journal of Her Trip to California, April 12, 1860."

Mother gave me this journal so I could record our travels to California. She said it would be a great adventure. She tries hard to be cheerful, but I know she doesn't want to go either. Father is dragging us off to the wilderness. The only clothes I had room to bring are the blue calico dress I'm wearing now, one other, a petticoat, two camisoles, pantaloons, and white cotton stockings. I guess they'll be mighty dingy by the end of the trip.

I don't want to go to California. Father says the journey will cost us nearly $1000! I love our farm here in Missouri. But Father says that there might be a war between the northern and southern states, and he wants to be far away when it starts. And Uncle Cyrus and Aunt Cora keep writing about how mild the winters are and how rich the soil is in Wheatland. They made the journey five years ago. But I don't see the rest of the neighbors picking up and taking off for California! Carrie's family certainly isn't. I don't know what I will do without Carrie. She's my best friend.

Besides, there's nothing for me to do in California. At home, I was the best student in my eighth grade graduating class. I always helped with the young'uns in our schoolhouse, so my teacher asked me to stay in Greenwood and be her assistant. Carrie said I could live with her, but Father said no. He said I was too young to be on my own—that I'm a member of this family, and we're all going to California whether we like it or not. He says I'll thank him later on.

Lucy stuck her pencil in her pocket and closed her journal. It was late afternoon now, and they had traveled the whole day with only short rests for the animals. Lucy shifted on the bag of feed. She could feel the patterns where the folds of the bag had dug into her legs.

She peered out the back of the wagon at Dandelion. The cow looked tired. Lucy was glad not to have to walk so far, although her father had said they might walk beside the wagon, once they were traveling with the wagon train. *Actually,* she thought, *it might be nice to walk in the fresh air all day.*

"This looks like a good place to camp for the night," Mr. Scott called, looking back into the wagon. In the late afternoon sunlight, his red beard looked like it was on fire. He slowed the horses to a stop in a grove of tall trees, their leaves just starting to bud. Green grass stretched to a quiet stream.

Lucy tumbled out of the wagon, stretching her stiff legs. Frank raced off to the trees. "Come back here, Boy!" called Mr. Scott. "Your mother needs your help! Julia, you help, too."

Lucy didn't need to be told to help. By the time she had brought water from the stream, her father had started a fire. Her mother put a metal frame over the fire and hung a pot from it. She put a little smoked meat and vegetables from home into the pot. Smoke billowed. Cooking over the fire was going to take some getting used to. At home, they cooked on a wood stove.

Mr. Scott showed Frank and Lucy how to put up the tent they would all sleep in. First he pegged down the four corners. Then he got the poles out of the wagon, one for the front and the other for the back of the tent. "Will we have to do this every night, Father?" Frank asked as he pounded the poles into the ground with the blunt end of an ax.

Mr. Scott grinned. "Yep. At least 'till it gets warmer. Then you can roll up in your quilt and sleep on the ground."

Lucy grimaced. "I don't want to sleep on the ground. What if there are snakes?"

"There are plenty of critters out here. We'll just have to get used to them," her father said. Frank pulled the canvas tight, while Mr. Scott put a rope over each pole and attached it to the pegs in the ground. The tent was ready.

Mr. Scott went to the wagon and got the trail guide, which had been prepared by pioneers who had already made the trip to California. He sat on a log by the fire. "Come see where we are going," he called, opening the map that was in the trail guide.

Lucy plopped down on the log beside him with a sigh. He smiled. "Well, if I've got to go, I might as well know where we're going," she muttered.

Mr. Scott ran his finger along a line that represented the road from Greenwood to Independence, Missouri. "We'll meet up with the rest of the wagon train in Independence tomorrow morning. We could have gotten there tonight, but I didn't want to push it this early in the journey."

"How many other wagons are going?" Lucy asked.

"I'm not sure," her father said. "Around forty."

That sounded like a lot of people to Lucy. Maybe there would be someone her age. "Where is Wheatland?" she asked.

"Here's Sacramento." Mr. Scott pointed it out on the map. "Wheatland is about twenty-five miles northeast—almost 2000 miles from Independence."

"I wonder if they need teachers there?" Lucy thought out loud.

"Could be," he said. "Hey, look—Mother's done with our stew." Raising his voice, he called, "Frank, dinner time!"

Mrs. Scott wiped her smoky face on her sleeve. "I'm afraid it's not very good." She paused. "I miss my nice kitchen, but the fire will do us just fine."

The firelight flickered over their exhausted faces as they ate silently. Afterward, Mrs. Scott and Lucy scoured the dirty dishes with ashes. They would rinse them in the stream tomorrow. Wrapping themselves in quilts, the family snuggled down in the tent. It was a tight fit for the five of them, but Mr. Scott started snoring right away.

Lucy stared into the darkness. The ground was cold, even though she was pressed up against warm bodies. She felt squashed. She could hardly turn over without rolling on top of Frank. She thought of her comfortable attic room at home and the feather bed she had shared with Julia, and tried to go to sleep.

*　　*　　*

Lucy was walking beside the wagon when they arrived in Independence the next morning. She'd never been in such a big town before, though her father had told her stories of his trips to Independence. The dirt streets were crowded with wagons, mules, oxen, and people. Wagon wheels squeaked, mules brayed, and men shouted. The hammering of blacksmiths filled the air. Lucy put her hands over her ears; the noise was deafening.

"Look at all the wagons," said Frank. "They're just like ours. The white tops look like sails."

"That's why they're called prairie schooners," said Mr. Scott from the front of the wagon.

"What's a schooner?" Frank asked.

"It's a boat with big sails," said Lucy.

"And our wagon is caulked to be as watertight as a ship," Mr. Scott added.

He pulled the wagon into a grassy field outside of town, where hundreds of other covered wagons already dotted the landscape. Men, women, and children wandered among them.

"I wonder which of these people will be in our wagon train?" Lucy said to Frank. She watched two tall young men, not much older than herself, walk briskly toward the middle of the camp and disappear behind a wagon. They looked a lot alike, both blond, except one had a small mustache and one didn't. *I hope they're traveling with us*, she thought. Boys her own age would make the journey bearable.

9

TWO

THERE WAS A LOT TO DO BEFORE THE WAG-
ons would be ready to leave Independence and
begin the journey along the California Trail. After they
arrived, Mr. Scott announced, "I need to go find
Colonel Alexander. He was the leader of Cyrus's wagon
train and he's leading this one. I need his advice on
buying oxen to pull our wagon."

"Can't our horses pull the wagon?" asked Lucy.
"We won't leave them behind, will we?"

"No, we can ride them or tie them behind the
wagon with Dandelion. But we need some strong
oxen to get across the mountains."

"Can I go look around?" Frank broke in.

"Yes," Mr. Scott said, "but take Julia along. And
don't get lost." Frank scampered off, towing Julia
behind him. Lucy hesitated. She knew her mother
probably needed her help.

Mrs. Scott smiled. "I know you're curious. Why
don't you go into town and pick up five pounds of
bacon at the general store? This will be our last
chance to buy supplies for a while, and it will give
you a chance to look around, too."

"Thank you, Mother," said Lucy, grateful that she

could explore a little. She felt happier than she had since leaving home. She was curious to see what Independence was like. She had never been this far from Greenwood before. She strolled up the dirt road into town, peering into the barber shops, black-smith shops, and saloons. Bales and barrels of food, hardware, and cloth were stacked on porches and in the streets in front of the wooden buildings. The streets were so crowded that the wagons, creaking slowly through town, could hardly move. Merchants in high hats rubbed shoulders with mountain men in buckskins carrying pelts for sale. Independence was the launching point for the West, a last stop for supplies for all the wagon trains.

After asking a few people, she found a building with a wooden sign over the door that read, "General Store." A hand-lettered sign in the window read, "Get Your Supplies Here."

Lucy stepped inside, where it was dark compared to the sunlit street. She blinked and saw the outline of a man behind a counter. "How can I help you, lit-tle lady?" the shape said.

"I need five pounds of salted bacon, please," Lucy said as her eyes adjusted to the dimness. While the man got the bacon, Lucy looked at the tall shelves filled with crackers, flour, pins, thread, paper, and pencils. On the walls were horse bridles, rope, rifles, and ammunition. The store was much bigger than the general store in Greenwood. When the storekeeper gave her the bacon wrapped in brown paper, Lucy paid him and took the bacon in both arms.

As she was struggling to open the door, it was pulled open from the outside. A tall young man with a small blond mustache held it for her. He was the one she had seen the day before.

"Thank you," she said shyly. The young man was nice-looking and his mustache gave him a dashing air. Behind him was the fellow who had to be his brother. They looked alike, except for the mustache.

"My pleasure," said the one who had opened the door. "Are you Lucy Scott?"

Lucy was startled. "Yes, I am! But how do you know my name?"

"We're Colonel Bill Alexander's nephews. I'm Seth Alexander and this is my brother, Aaron. We're helping our uncle with the wagon train." He closed the door behind her. "You're the person we're looking for. Your father wants you to show us where your wagon is, so we can check your supplies."

Lucy and the young men walked toward the campground. "Have you been to California before?" asked Lucy, staring at Seth's mustache.

"Yeah. We took the trail west five years ago when we were twelve." He grinned again. "If you didn't notice, we're twins."

Lucy looked over at Aaron, who walked quietly beside his brother. He nodded to her, then stopped. "Here, let me carry your parcel for you." He reached over to take the bundle of bacon. She gave it to him gratefully.

Seth continued to talk. "I think we traveled with your Uncle Cyrus and Aunt Cora. Now our family

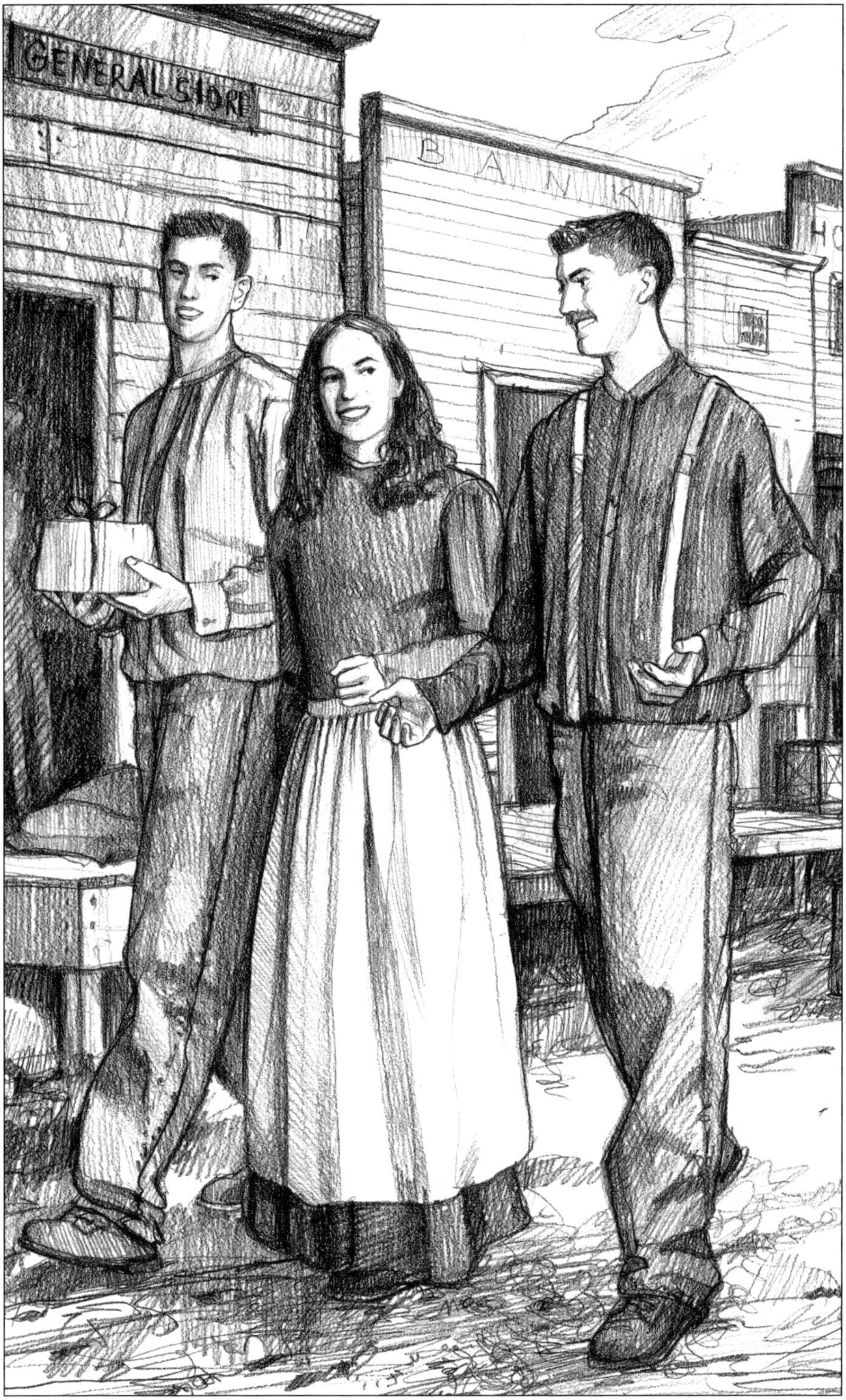
GENERAL STORE

owns a farm near Sacramento."

"Sacramento? That's close to where we're going. What's the trip like?" Lucy asked.

"It's long, dirty, and hot—not much water, but it can be exciting." Seth answered. "We usually meet quite a few Indians along the way." He grinned at Lucy's startled expression.

"They're mostly friendly," Aaron said quietly. He was silent for the rest of the walk to the wagon. Seth kept up a steady stream of friendly chatter. Lucy felt her heart flutter every time he grinned at her.

When they arrived at the Scotts' wagon, Lucy introduced the pair to her mother. "Thank you for carrying the bacon for Lucy," Mrs. Scott said to Aaron. She turned to Lucy with a disappointed look. "I meant to ask you to buy some vinegar and mustard, too, but I plumb forgot."

"I know where they sell it," said Aaron eagerly. "Do you want me to show you?"

"Thank you. Just let me get my sunbonnet. Lucy, please stay here and show Seth the wagon."

Seth laughed and shook his head as Aaron and Mrs. Scott walked away. "Aaron is so shy around girls that he'd rather help their mothers than stay and talk." Lucy blushed.

Seth smoothed his mustache, becoming businesslike. "Well, now, let's check your tools." He looked through the Scotts' tool chest and checked Mr. Scott's rifle. "It looks to me like you have all you need. You have bullets, a shovel, chains for the mountains, and plenty of rope."

He leaned against the wagon and looked at Lucy. "So, tell me, Lucy. What do you think about going to California?"

Lucy studied the ground for a minute and then looked up. "I don't want to go. I'd rather stay in Missouri and be a teacher, but I have to do what my father says." She looked down again.

Seth reached out and patted her shoulder. "Going to California is an adventure. You'll see."

"Maybe for you, but not for me," she murmured.

Seth cocked his head. "Hey, trust me. You'll like it once you get there." He caught her eyes. "I promise." The corners of his mouth twitched upwards. "But I've got to get going. See you around, Curly."

Lucy reached up to touch one of the dark curls that hung below her sunbonnet and watched him walk away until he disappeared behind a wagon. Then she crawled into the wagon and pulled out her journal. The trip was beginning to look better.

*   *   *

Four nights later, Lucy sat beside the wagon, writing again.

April 16, 1860. Today was our first day on the trail, and we're already in Kansas Territory. The past three days in Independence, everyone was so busy with preparations for the journey that I didn't get to talk to Seth or Aaron much. I saw them everywhere, though, helping get the wagon train together. They are both nice boys, but I like Seth better. He's friendlier, and the mustache makes him look grown up. They're seventeen now—that's only three years older than I am.

Before we left Independence, Father bought six oxen to pull the wagon. Frank and I got to ride the horses beside the wagon. Even so, I'm exhausted now. Colonel Alexander rides at the head of the line on his gray mare. Colonel Alexander says that during the journey the wagons will rotate places so the rest of us don't have to eat the dust from the lead wagon the entire summer.

There are some other families with children the same age as Frank and Julia, but I haven't seen any girls my age. There is one girl named Sabrina, who is probably nineteen. She is married, and I know it's not proper to talk about this, but I think she is expecting a baby. Maybe she will be a friend.

A doctor and his wife are also with us. They don't have any children, but they have two wagons. Mrs. Gray, the doctor's wife, is very fashionable. She wears bloomers and looks like a fashion plate in one of Mother's magazines. She wears a short, full skirt over the bloomers, which come down to her ankles. Mother makes such a fuss about me being modest when I get in and out of the wagon, but I don't show any more of my legs than Mrs. Gray does.

Of course Father was shocked when he saw her. "What can the doctor be thinking to let his wife wear such an outlandish outfit? A woman in pants!" he said in that disapproving way he has. Well, I think it would be a lot easier to live on the trail in bloomers.

For one thing, it would be easier to get in and out of the wagons. I also wish I had a straw hat like Mrs. Gray instead of a sunbonnet. I look like a little girl in this thing, and I want Seth to think I'm grown up. I wonder what Carrie would think of Seth?

We covered fifteen miles today before stopping at four o'clock. Colonel Alexander showed us how to make a circle, called a corral, with the wagons. We will eat, sleep, and keep the animals inside the circle for safety. The men will take turns guarding the livestock and wagons all night. Tonight, we built fires inside the circle next to our wagons. It's cozy. You can see all the pioneers sitting at their fires. Now Father is over playing chess with Dr. Gray, and Mother is with Frank and Julia visiting another family. I can see Seth and Aaron by their campfire. I wonder if I dare go talk to them. Father and Mother don't approve of girls being alone with boys.

Lucy put down her pencil and made up her mind. She shyly walked toward their campfire. Aaron was bent over a guitar, picking out a few chords. Seth was whittling a piece of wood with his knife.

"Hey, Lucy," Seth called. "Come join us." Delighted, Lucy sat down next to him.

"You play the guitar?" Lucy asked Aaron.

"I don't play so well," he said, turning red.

"Yes, he does. He's a regular troubadour," said Seth. "Why don't you play something we can sing?"

"Oh, yes, please do," Lucy begged. She loved to sing.

Aaron smiled shyly at Lucy, and started playing "My Old Kentucky Home."

"Not that one," Seth interrupted. "Something cheerful. Do you know Mr. Stephen Foster's songs, Lucy?"

"I love them!" she smiled back at him. "Let's sing them." Her clear soprano joined Seth's firm baritone as Aaron played "Camptown Races" and "Beautiful Dreamer." Dusk deepened and the campfire burned low. Lucy moved a little closer to Seth.

She stood up when the stars began to come out. "I'd better go," she said regretfully.

"I'll walk you back to your wagon, Lucy," Seth volunteered, standing.

Aaron looked up from the fire. "We've got to check on the horses, Seth. It's close enough that Lucy can walk back alone."

"True," Seth said. "Well, good night, Curly." He reached out and tugged at a curl.

Lucy giggled and turned to walk to her wagon. *Seth fancies me. I know he does!* she thought.

THREE

*A*PRIL 27, 1860. WE'VE BEEN ALMOST A *fortnight on the trail now. Within a couple of days we should be at Alcove Spring, where we shall cross the Big Blue River. Each morning at sunrise, Colonel Alexander plays a wake-up call on his bugle. I get up, dress, and roll up the quilts, while Father stows our tent, hitches the oxen, and ties the horses and cow to the wagon. I help Mother cook a breakfast of flapjacks or stewed apples and coffee. After we clean the dishes, we start on the road. The trail never changes, except that when it rains it gets very muddy. It is worn in ruts from all the wagons that have come before.*

The men drive the wagons. Most of the women sit on the wagon seats with their husbands while they hold babies or knit. Because the wagons are so crowded, only the younger children ride in them. The rest of us walk, except, of course, when it rains, and then we all pile in. Today, I had a really bad blister on my heel, so Father let Frank and me ride the horses. When we walk, we have no trouble keeping up with the wagons because we usually only travel about fifteen or twenty miles a day. Our feet always ache at the end of the day. Sometimes I walk with Sabrina or

Mrs. Gray, so I am getting to know them. Sabrina is very sweet. Mrs. Gray is very sophisticated.

Seth, Aaron, and Colonel Alexander ride along-side the wagons to keep us together. Seth usually stops and chats for a minute as he rides by, but Aaron never does. I think Aaron is just shy, but his brother acts nicer. Sometimes, I think Seth must fancy me. But other times, I'm not sure. I want to get to know him better, but he's always so busy helping his uncle that we haven't had much time together.

Every day at noon, we stop for "nooning." I'm already tired of the same cold lunch every day: boiled beans, dried beef, or salted bacon with crackers and water. At least we have butter to put on the crackers, and I don't have to churn anymore! Now I put Dandelion's milk in the churn, tie it to the back of the wagon before we set off, and the rocking of the wagon churns it to butter!

At noon the oxen are unhitched from the wagon so they can graze. They have wooden yokes around their necks that keep them together. It takes a long time to put the heavy yoke across their necks and slip the hickory oxbows up and set the pegs, so Father does this only in the morning. The oxen stay yoked until we stop for the night.

Evenings are best. After the oxen circle the wagons for the night, we all have chores. Frank feeds the ani-mals. Father milks Dandelion while Julia gathers sticks for the fire. Mother and I cook dinner and clean up afterwards. Frank and I can put up the tent quickly now.

When all the chores are done, I teach games to

Julia and the other children or write in my journal. Sometimes I work with Julia in her beginning reader. She's a quick learner. I keep hoping Seth will stop by in the evening, but so far he hasn't. I guess he's too busy. That first night, when Aaron played the guitar and we both sang, was mighty nice. But I best not go over to their campfire uninvited. What if they don't want me there at all but are just being nice? Besides, Father told me I should ask him before I go over.

Lucy looked up from her diary restlessly. The sun was low on the horizon, and the evening was the warmest yet this spring. She wanted to get out of camp. Perhaps Sabrina would go on a walk with her to pick some blue lupine.

Sabrina looked tired, and her stomach was just beginning to bulge beneath her apron, but she agreed eagerly. "Long as we don't go too far from the camp," she said.

The two girls walked along the trail they would travel tomorrow. Lucy kicked absently at the ruts left from hundreds of wagon trains. The ruts stretched far ahead of the camp, heading west.

"It's strange to see such fertile land and no farms," Lucy said, staring at the flat stretch of gently waving grasses before them. Sabrina smiled and said nothing, tucking a strand of black hair behind her ears. She gazed west, too.

"Do you want to go to California?" Lucy asked softly. "Or are you like me and don't have anything to say about it?"

"Oh, I want to go," Sabrina said, turning to look at Lucy. She smiled. "Tom started talking about California before we were married. I'm looking forward to the good weather and the cheap land, so we can have our own farm. If war comes, we'll be far away, and Tom won't have to fight." She gazed at the fantastic sunset, flaming across the western sky. "We had to wait until we'd saved enough money for a wagon and supplies before we could start. By the time we saved the money and our plans were made, I—" Sabrina paused and blushed, looking ruefully at her softly swelling stomach. "I was expecting our baby. But we decided it was now or never."

She stopped to pick a flower and then looked earnestly into Lucy's blue eyes. "Lucy, I don't want to have my baby on the trail. I've heard stories about women having babies with no one to help them." Sabrina looked worried. "I know we have a doctor in this train, but we've just got to get to California before my baby is born."

Lucy touched Sabrina's hand. "I'm sure we will get to California before your time," she murmured. Sabrina smiled, and they went back to camp, but Lucy couldn't stop thinking about their conversation. Sabrina had more reasons to dread this trip than she did, yet she still wanted to go.

April 30, Monday. We have arrived at Alcove Spring, where we shall wait a few days for the water to go down before we cross the Big Blue River. This is the most beautiful place I have ever seen, with a cold, clear spring spilling over a ledge to make a waterfall. There are also hills and trees. Father says the grazing is good. I wish we could just stay here. We have all refilled our water barrels. The water is frigid, but Sabrina and I waded for a few minutes to wash our feet until we got too cold. Seth and Aaron waded, too, and Seth splashed water on me. It was icy cold, but I didn't mind. He MUST fancy me. Maybe Seth won't be so busy the next few days and we'll have a chance to visit.

"Isn't it beautiful here?" Mrs. Scott exclaimed as she soaked the dirt-crusted clothes in a wooden tub. "It's so hard to wash when we are moving all day."

Lucy helped her spread the clothes on the prairie grass to dry. It felt nice to wear a clean dress. Her other dress was soaking in the tub now.

"Why don't you run along?" Mrs. Scott said, looking up. "I'm mostly done washing."

Lucy hugged her mother happily. "Thank you, Mother. I'm going to pick some wildflowers. I won't go far."

Spring was in full bloom. The prairie grass along the Big Blue had a blue tint to it in the bright sun, and flowers bloomed everywhere. The warm sun felt good on Lucy's back. She took off her sunbonnet and fanned at the mosquitoes. Climbing one low hill after another, she picked sprigs of yellow mustard blossoms here and there, daydreaming that an Indian war party had kidnapped her. All was hopeless until Seth galloped to her rescue.

It was beginning to get hot. Lucy wandered into a shady grove of trees and searched for flowers until she noticed that the sun was getting low on the horizon. She knew she should start back. She walked back the way she had come, but nothing looked familiar. Lucy stopped. Suddenly she realized she didn't know where she was. She hadn't paid attention to where she was walking.

What should she do? Scanning the horizon for some sign of the camp, she turned and walked back to the grove of trees. Clouds were beginning to mass in gray heaps and cover the sun, which was sinking quickly behind the hills.

Lucy put her sunbonnet back on. She wished she had brought her shawl. She knew the best thing to do when you were lost was stay where you were, but this country was so empty. There were no roads or people to help her like there were back home. No one knew which way she had gone. How would she get back? Why had she been so careless?

The sky grew darker and darker. The wind began to blow fiercely. Lucy shivered against a tree. She wanted to cry. She wished Seth would come. Or somebody. Anybody. How would they find her? The prairie was so huge.

She thought she heard a horse's hooves. "Help!" she cried, her skirts flapping wildly in the wind. "Please, help me!" But the sound died away, and all was quiet.

A raindrop fell, and then another. Lucy huddled in the small grove, but the trees were little protection from the cold, stinging rain. She heard the hooves again. This time they were louder and coming closer. Lucy jumped up and waved her hands. "I'm here! Please, help me!"

A horse crashed through the underbrush. She recognized a tall figure on the horse. *It must be Seth, just like in my daydream*, she thought excitedly.

"Lucy! What are you doing here?" a voice shouted over the wind. It belonged to Aaron.

"Oh, Aaron! I'm so glad to see you. I don't know how to get back. I went for a walk and got lost." Lucy shivered. "Did you come looking for me?"

"No, I was out for a ride," Aaron said, quickly dismounting. He helped her put her left foot in the stirrup and swing her right leg over the saddle. Then he swung up behind her. He put his arms around Lucy to hold the reins. "Let's hurry back to the wagons."

Aaron's strong back protected her from much of the slanting rain. His chin softly touched the side of her head, and she could smell his buckskin jacket. They rode quickly through the rain, but he held her securely on the saddle.

It didn't take long to get back to the wagon camp near the spring. All the pioneers huddled inside the wagons trying to keep dry. "I'll get off here," she said to Aaron, as they drew up outside her wagon. But as she dismounted, her foot caught in the stirrup and she fell forward. Aaron awkwardly grabbed at her pinafore. With a little shriek, Lucy pitched forward on her hands and knees into the mud. Mr. Scott came running around the side of the wagon.

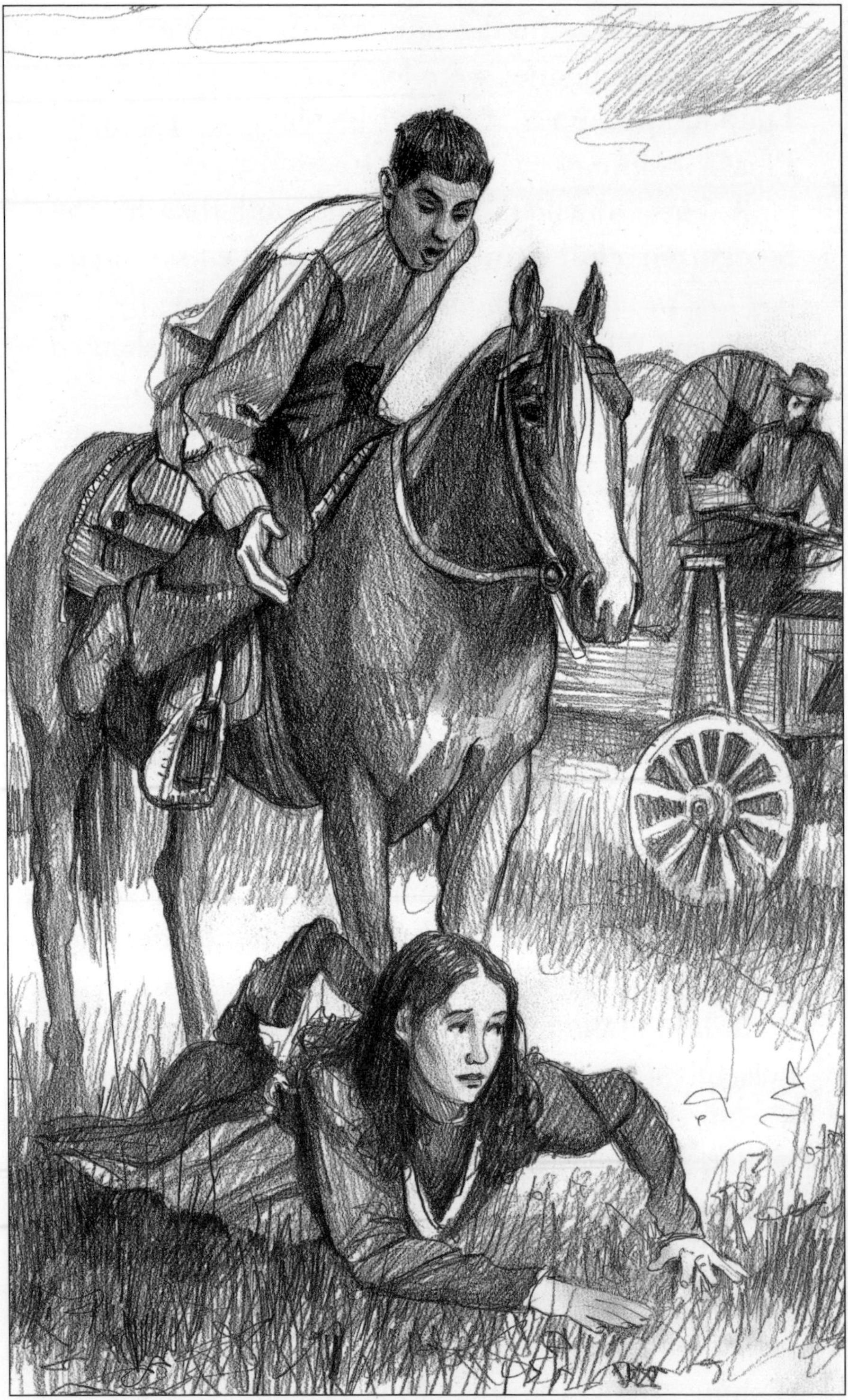

"Lucy!"

She looked up from the mud. Aaron sat up in the saddle awkwardly.

"Where have you been, girl? Your mother's been half-sick with worry." Mr. Scott tugged on his beard angrily. Lucy stood up.

"I'm sorry, Father. I got lost and—"

"You might have been hurt—or worse!" he said angrily, grabbing one of Lucy's muddy elbows.

"But Father—"

"Get in the wagon this minute, young lady." Lucy began to cry.

Aaron turned and rode away hurriedly.

Mr. Scott steered her to the wagon roughly and growled to his wife, "Your daughter is a muddy mess. She needs to pay more mind to her surroundings."

In the wagon, Mrs. Scott looked at Lucy's muddy dress dismally.

"I'm sorry, Mother" Lucy cried. "I got lost and it started to rain, and I didn't know how to get back—"

"More washing," Lucy's mother sighed wearily. "I wish you'd been more careful, Lucy."

Her father was still so angry he didn't say a word. Finally he barked, "I just hope she doesn't catch pneumonia. Get her out of those wet clothes, Mother. Miss Lucy shall have no supper tonight."

FOUR

NO ONE GOT ANY SUPPER THAT NIGHT. The rain came down in sheets, while Lucy's family huddled in the middle of the wagon to keep warm; there was no room to lay out bedrolls. Lucy pressed up against her brother and sister and thought of Aaron riding into the grove to find her. She smiled as she fell asleep.

She woke at first light, shivering with cold, her back aching, and her stomach empty. The rain had leaked in above the sideboards of the wagon and through the front opening. All their blankets were damp.

Mrs. Scott tried to cook a breakfast of bacon and coffee in the rain, but it didn't work. The smoky fire kept going out. They climbed back into the wagon and ate crackers and butter.

Rain fell all morning. Lucy felt sick and damp and miserable. Frank couldn't sit still and kept fidgeting. Mr. Scott sat huddled with the rest of them, coughing now and then. Mrs. Scott looked worn out. They couldn't cross the Big Blue River in this weather, so they would just have to wait.

Julia was pale, and she looked sick, too. Lucy held out one arm and Julia crawled into it, clutching her rag doll. She stuck her braid in her mouth and fell asleep. Mrs. Scott caught Lucy's eye and nodded approvingly. Lucy leaned against the damp side of the wagon and thought about last night. She was humiliated that her father had made a scene in front of Aaron. How could she ever face Aaron again? Her father was so stern sometimes.

Lucy fell into a daydream of being back on the horse with Aaron, his chin brushing the back of her head. He was awfully nice. But she was sweet on Seth, not his brother. And Aaron would have saved anyone lost in that storm. She grew warm with Julia asleep on her lap. Lucy's head slowly nodded down over her sister's.

She woke to a blinding flash and a crack louder than a gunshot, followed by an earsplitting peal of thunder. Outside the wagon, there was a confused scramble of screams and shouts. "What is it?" she asked groggily. Mr. Scott jumped over the wagon seat and leapt out of sight. A few minutes later there was a thumping on the canvas top and cracking sounds on the wooden wheels; it sounded like someone was throwing rocks at the wagon. Soon after, Mr. Scott squeezed back into the wagon, gasping. "Lightning struck one of Doc Gray's wagons. We were trying to put out the fire when the hail started. Those hailstones are as big as hen's eggs. I've never seen them so big. I reckon the rain will put out the fire, but those hailstones can do just as much damage."

Lucy shivered. She could see the canvas ceiling

sagging under the weight of the hailstones. "Are the Grays all right?"

"They're safe but pretty scared. Mrs. Gray is wailing like a banshee, saying she wants to go home."

I wouldn't mind doing that myself, Lucy thought, biting her lip. When the hail stopped, she tentatively lifted the canvas flap covering the back opening. Frank jumped out of the wagon and started throwing hailstones into the woods. "Look, Lucy, look how big they are!" he shouted, playing catch with his friend John.

Lucy stepped out of the wagon and gingerly made her way through the uneven layer of hailstones on the ground. Sabrina's wagon top had a big hole in it. Another family's canvas water bucket was ruined. Dr. Gray stood with Colonel Alexander, staring morosely at his charred and blackened wagon. The canvas top had been destroyed as well as most of the furniture inside, but the wagon was still usable. They discussed whether they could find more canvas at another stop along the way. Mrs. Gray sat on the wagon seat of their other wagon, sobbing quietly on Mrs. Scott's shoulder. "I want to go home. We never should have tried to go to California. My furniture—we could have been killed."

"It will be all right," Lucy's mother comforted.

Lucy knew that Dr. Gray wouldn't turn back now. They would all have to do the best they could to get to California safely. She glanced over to where Seth and Aaron were helping someone repair a damaged wagon top. If they could stick it out, so could she.

May 2, 1860. Wednesday. Since the storm, Father and I are getting along better. He hasn't mentioned Monday night when I got lost, and we've been reading the trail guide together. We have to wait a few more days here at Alcove Spring for the river to go down after that storm. I'm glad we had time to wash my dress again. Mother made me do it myself this time. I don't know when I started to, but right now, I'm rather enjoying myself. This is an adventure just like Seth said it would be. Sometimes I think about how I'll tell my grandchildren about this journey. Sometimes I daydream about marrying Seth. Mrs. Lucy Alexander. Doesn't that sound nice? He came by today and said Aaron told him about my mishap. He told me that if I come by their campfire tonight, he'll show me some special Indian signs to keep me from getting lost again. Father and Mother said I may go. Maybe if I go to his campfire, I'll see Aaron. I think Aaron has been avoiding me. He turns red every time he sees me now. He must be embarrassed because Father yelled at me in front of him. That was so humiliating!

When her chores were done for the day, Lucy washed her face and hands, combed her dark curls, and wiped off her muddy shoes before she walked over to the boys' wagon. Seth was alone when she got there.

"Aaron has guard duty tonight," said Seth. "Sit here next to me, and I'll show you how to make the signs that will keep you from getting lost."

Lucy sat on the log beside Seth and watched him pick up a stick and lay it on the ground. His arms were strong and tanned. She could see his muscles where his sleeves were rolled up.

"Take a long stick and lay it like this, pointing the way you are going." Seth put a stone on either side of the stick. "See, these stones show that it isn't just an ordinary stick. Then, put a shorter stick at a right angle to point the way you plan to go. If you do this often while you are walking, you won't get lost." He sat back and grinned at her. "Ok, now show me how you do a left turn, Curly."

Lucy did exactly what Seth had taught her. They practiced some more. When the lesson was over, Seth talked about the trip west. He talked about horses, deserts, and Indians.

Too soon, Lucy realized that it was time for her to leave. Most of the pioneers were quiet in their bedrolls. "I'd better go now," she said. "Thank you, Seth. I'm sure I won't get lost again."

"I'm sure you won't, either. Just make those signs if you get lost on the way back to your wagon," Seth grinned. "Good night, Curly."

*   *   *

By Saturday, the Big Blue River had receded enough for the wagon train to cross. Colonel Alexander had the wagons cross in the afternoon because the water was warmer and the animals less frisky. He had all the livestock drink before starting, so they wouldn't stop to drink in the middle of the river. First, Seth and Aaron rode across to see how deep the water was and where the holes were. Then the wagons crossed one at a time so the boys could make sure they were safe. The oxen swam, and each wagon floated like a boat until it was safely on the other side.

"Come on, Lucy. It's our turn!" Frank shouted. Lucy carefully picked her way down the muddy bank to get into the wagon. Mr. Scott was driving the oxen, and Mrs. Scott sat beside him. Lucy sat in the middle of the wagon with Frank and Julia. The oxen walked down into the water. The wagon looked as though it were floating like a boat. Trickles of water came up through a few cracks in the boards. Lucy sat rigidly: What if they turned over? What if the wagon sank in the deeper water toward the middle of the river? Suddenly the wagon lurched to the left. One of the lead oxen had stepped into a hole. The oxen behind him tried to keep on going and the wagon swayed dangerously.

Pots and pans clanged together overhead and then fell off their hooks into the wagon bed. A small one hit Lucy in the head and she screamed.

Mr. Scott struggled to control the team. It seemed the whole wagon might tip over. "Hang on to Julia!" Lucy shouted to Frank. She was so scared she could hardly breathe. What if they tipped over into the water and drowned?

Suddenly at the back of the wagon, she saw

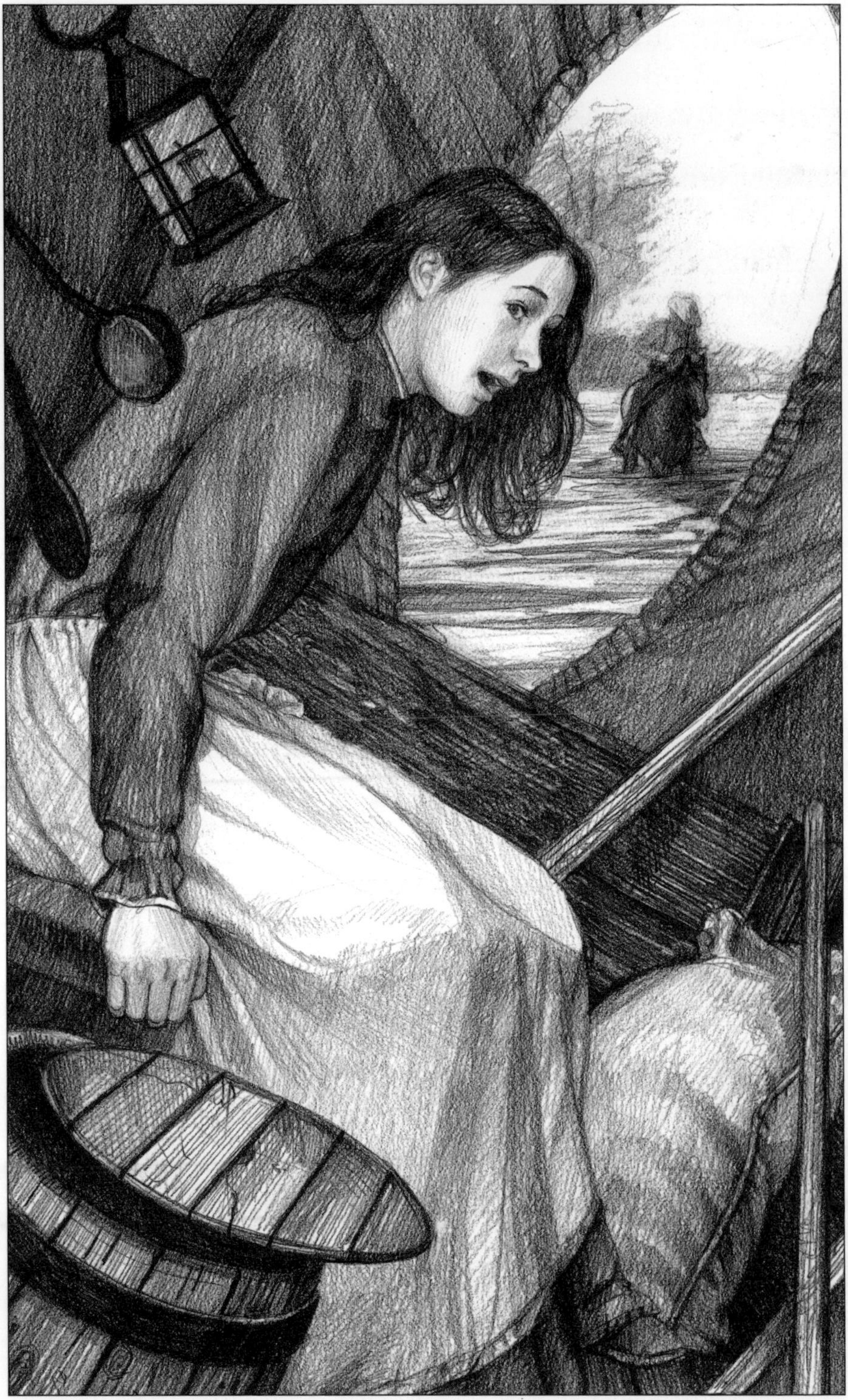

Aaron on his horse, wading alongside. "Lucy! Frank! Julia!" he yelled. "Move to the uphill side!" They scrambled up the slanted floor of the wagon and hung on to the sideboards. At the front of the wagon, Lucy saw Seth pulling on the reins of the lead ox. He led the frightened animal out of the hole and into the deeper water. The team began to swim, and the wagon leveled out.

Mr. and Mrs. Scott looked back into the wagon anxiously. "Lucy got an awful knock on the head," Frank said.

"Are you all right, Lucy?" Mr. Scott shouted back over the splashing of the animals and wagons.

She rubbed her sore head. "Yes, Father." She was still frightened, but now the oxen were swimming smoothly across the currents. Although the crossing seemed to take hours, finally the wagon wheels hit mud on the other side of the river, and the oxen pulled the wagon up the bank to level land. *I hope we don't have to cross any more rivers like this*, thought Lucy, as they waited the rest of the morning for the other wagons to cross. The plains stretched before them, the trail marked by wagon ruts pointing north and west.

FIVE

*M*AY 12, 1860. WE ARE ON THE PLAINS OF *Nebraska Territory now. At night packs of coyotes howl and yip at the moon. Julia cries when she hears them. It's an eerie sound, but I'm getting used to it. Nebraska Territory is hot and dusty except when it rains. It has rained twice this week, and the rain turns everything to mud. We passed a trading post a little way back, where Doc Gray bought a new canvas top for his wagon.*

The land is always the same—flat like a sea of tall grass. We never seem to make progress. It's almost like walking in place. We pass a lot of prairie dog villages. The prairie dogs dig holes that leave little mounds of dirt. Sometimes we see them poking their sweet little faces out, sniffing the air. Seth says that underneath there are cities of tunnels and prairie dogs. He says prairie dog stew is good eating.

Seth rides by the wagon and talks to me, but sometimes I don't see him for a day or two. I reckon he's busy. My face and hands are sunburned, even though I have started wearing my sunbonnet all the time like Mother says I should. I wonder if Seth has noticed.

Aaron came by our campfire last night and talked

with Father and Mother about the Indians hereabouts. He said we came into Indian Country on our first day out of Independence. I was surprised to learn that we have been passing through Pawnee hunting grounds, for we haven't seen any Indians at all so far. Aaron said many Indian tribes live in Nebraska Territory—the Arapaho, Cheyenne, Omaha, Sioux, and Oto. I've only heard bad things about Indians, but Aaron seems to like them. He told Father that if we stay clear and don't make trouble for ourselves, we should be safe. I'm still scared, though—I've heard stories about wagon trains that never made it to California or Oregon.

May 20, Sunday. Today we're resting, as we usually do on Sundays. We've been on the trail for over a month now. These past days, we've been traveling along the South Platte River. Colonel Alexander says the Platte is too thin to plow, too thick to drink, and too muddy to bathe in. It's shallow enough to wade in, though. In the middle are islands with cottonwood trees on them. We'll follow the river for about three hundred miles. Everyone is pleased because there is good grazing so far. Tonight we are camped at Fort Kearny, which is mostly a military outpost, but there are quite a few houses here too, some built of wood and some of sod. Father says it's easier for folks to build sod houses around here because there is so little wood. Mother bought fresh vegetables from some of the women who have gardens. We catch fish in the river by poking them with sharp sticks. Aaron says that's how Indians fish. Father is having some of the oxen re-shod by the local blacksmith. I wouldn't mind staying here longer, but we have to move on.

June 1. Our journey continues. The land here is mostly flat, dry, and covered with alkali pools that Seth calls "bitter water." Oxen from one of the other wagons got terribly sick after drinking from them. So now we know better. Fortunately, the Platte, though muddy, is a steady water supply for the animals. But we keep a lookout for water moccasins when we wade in. They are poisonous!

There are no twigs to make Seth's signs or to gather for firewood. So Julia, Frank, and I have to gather buffalo chips for fires. The chips are dried buffalo dung. They don't smell too bad and their smoke keeps mosquitoes away, but it takes a basketful to make a good fire. The men and older boys go out hunting off the trail. Colonel Alexander told us this country was covered with buffalo—well, he calls them bison—when he passed through five years ago. He said the Pawnee value the buffalo highly. We have seen very few of the animals so far. They have not been close enough to shoot. But there is plenty of other game. Our oxen constantly scare up pheasants out of the tall grass, and the birds fly up into the air with a loud whirring sound. We ate grouse last evening for supper. Along the river are many wild ducks and geese, which make for good eating. There is another kind of bird—a crane—with long legs and a long, narrow bill. They look very awkward when they land in the water.

I get dirtier everyday. Seth stops by and talks a lot.

Julia is coming along well with her reading. I have been helping her each day.

June 7. The land is getting hillier. We are coming into sight of some interesting rock formations. Courthouse Rock looks like a big building. Mrs. Gray says they have courthouses just like it back east where she used to live. There's another one called Chimney Rock that looks like a big chimney. Both rock formations are far off now. Julia read a hard passage in her primer today. Mother says I'm a good teacher.

The next day, as Lucy walked beside Sabrina, they gazed at Courthouse Rock. "I wonder if we could walk over and see those rocks?" Lucy said.

"They don't look so far away," Sabrina replied. "Why don't you ask Aaron?" She nodded past Lucy.

Lucy looked up and saw Aaron riding alongside them. She blushed.

"Aaron," called Sabrina. "How long do you think it would take Lucy to walk to Courthouse Rock?"

Aaron slowed his horse and smiled, shyly avoiding Lucy's eyes. "Seth and I tried to climb that rock on our first trip. It's not as close as it looks. How far off do you think it is?"

"About half a mile?" guessed Sabrina. Lucy nodded.

"Nope, it's about five miles."

"Oh," said Lucy disappointed. "I wanted to see it up close."

"There's an old Indian legend," Aaron said, "that there were once some Pawnee warriors who were besieged on top of that rock by some of their enemy, the Sioux. One of the Pawnee had a dream one night that showed him a secret trail down the back side of the rock. The young men escaped, but the old men decided to stay up there to sing and keep the fires burning so the Sioux would think they were all still trapped. Some say that if you camp near the rock, you can still hear the old warriors singing."

Aaron's blond hair lifted in the light breeze as he gazed toward the rock. He looked back at Lucy, embarrassed. "Of course, it's just the wind people hear, soughing through the rocks."

Lucy's skin prickled. "I've always been scared of Indians. To think that they could be out there now, where we can't see them—"

"They lived on this land thousands of years before we knew anything about it," Aaron interrupted forcefully. He turned red. "Sorry. I didn't mean to shout. It's just that I—I, uh—I need to keep moving. See you around." He spurred his horse forward.

Lucy watched him ride away and shook her head. Sabrina looked sideways at her; "He's a nice boy, isn't he?"

Lucy looked at her, "Yes, he's nice." She twirled her sunbonnet strings. "But he's strange, too. Since we've been on the trail that's the most I've heard him say."

Sabrina smiled. "Seems to me his brother does plenty of talking for both of them."

June 9. Last night we camped near Chimney Rock. The trail guide says it is around 500 feet tall!

Today, we're camping near Scott's Bluff, a huge rock that looks like a castle. Seth teased me that it was named for our family, but then he was serious and said it was actually named for a man who died there. We have been steadily climbing in elevation. There are some French fur traders' cabins and an Indian camp nearby. I'm still afraid Indians might attack us. I've thought about what Aaron said—how the Indians have lived here for a long, long time. I'd like to ask him some more about that, but he's been avoiding me. He is awfully shy.

June 12. We've arrived at Fort Laramie in Wyoming Territory. It's a trading post and an army base. There's an adobe fort and a "tent city" situated in the fork where the Laramie and Platte Rivers meet, and a toll bridge across the Laramie, which we will take tomorrow. It is so nice to come to this civilized place—the first real settlement in weeks. When Father and I studied the map, we saw that we are still closer to Independence than to California. Such a long journey! We've traveled more than 500 miles!

Today, Mother and I spent the afternoon airing the wagon. We unpacked it, checked all our provisions and then repacked it. We've filled the barrels with fresh water for the trip ahead and done our washing. The rest of the day, I looked around Fort Laramie.

I was shocked when Mother and I went to the store. The shopkeeper tried to sell us sugar for $1.50 a cup! He sells flour for $1.50 per pint. I have never heard of such high prices. Mother says the shopkeeper knows he has *travelers in a bind and can charge what he pleases. Well, we don't need his food. We still have plenty packed in our wagon. In fact, Father said some in our train are talking of dumping some of their goods here at Fort Laramie, as the soldiers have told them the trail ahead is very rough. That worries me.*

Outside the fort are quite a few Indian wigwams. I saw Aaron buying some moccasins from some Indians. He looked more comfortable with them than with the people in our wagon train.

In the evening, Lucy walked with her family to visit the soldiers. Mr. and Mrs. Scott talked with the officers on the porch of the headquarters, while Seth and Aaron joined the young enlisted men on the parade ground. Many of the soldiers looked as young as Seth and Aaron. Lucy wished she could go down and join them, but she felt awkward. Besides, she knew her father and mother didn't like her joining the young men without an invitation.

She stood alone, rubbing the toe of her worn shoe over the cracks in the brick sidewalk. She gazed at the sunset on the horizon and then glanced over at the group of boys. Aaron was looking at her.

"Lucy!" yelled Seth. "Come join us. There's somebody I want you to meet."

That was an invitation. Lucy glanced sideways at her father and slipped away. "Lucy," Seth smoothed his moustache and put his hand on the shoulder of a young soldier, "This is Private Richard Willard. He's from Missouri, too, and he's homesick."

"Pleased to make your acquaintance," the boy said politely.

"Where in Missouri are you from?" Lucy asked.

The young soldier ducked his head. He seemed almost as shy as Aaron did. "Near Independence—Greenwood."

"That's where I'm from!" Lucy exclaimed. It turned out Richard knew some of the same people she did. They chatted happily. Lucy sneaked a glance at Seth, who was talking animatedly to the other soldiers. Aaron stood with his hands in his pockets watching the sunset. His guitar hung from a strap on his back.

Finally, Seth clapped his hands. "Fellows, gather 'round. Let's have a sing-along."

Aaron strummed a chord, and Richard pulled a harmonica out of his pocket and began to play with him. The group sang "O Susanna," "Skip to My Lou," and "Sweet Betsy From Pike." Lucy couldn't remember the last time she'd had so much fun.

*   *   *

The wagon train rolled on, following the ruts cut into the soil by thousands of wagons before them. A promise unfolded with each mile: California.

One late afternoon after the wagons were circled for the night, Lucy thought she heard a rumble of thunder. She peered at the flat horizon. The air was so clear that she could see for miles. "Look, Frank," she said. "Do you see that dusty cloud up ahead?"

It was like a brown fog rolling across the horizon.

The cloud grew bigger. The ground rumbled. "Father come look at this," called Frank.

Mr. Scott came around the side of the wagon. "Could those be buffalo? Frank, go ask Colonel Alexander what he thinks, hurry!"

A few minutes later the colonel hurried over. "They're buffalo, all right. Some hunters must have shot one and started a stampede. Buffalo will run until they are tired out. Looks like they are coming right for us. Frank, run call all the men to bring their rifles and come fast. Lucy, tell all the women and children to stay inside the corral. Have them build up the fires with anything they can find. Scream as loud as you can. Should scare the buffalo."

Now Lucy could see the herd clearly. The buffalo were bigger than cows, with humped backs and shaggy brown coats. It looked like there were thousands of them. The thundering sound of their hooves grew louder and the ground trembled. Lucy felt as if her feet were frozen to the ground.

"Come on, girl," Colonel Alexander shouted. "Move it! Move! Move!"

Lucy raced toward the wagons crying, "Build the fires!" Within moments the women were stoking the blazing fires. The screams of children filled the air. Lucy's heart beat in her throat. She stood beside Frank shouting at the top of her lungs. Colonel Alexander shouted instructions to the crowd of men. They loaded their rifles and shot into the sky. Thousands of buffalo feet pounded over the ground as the men fired and

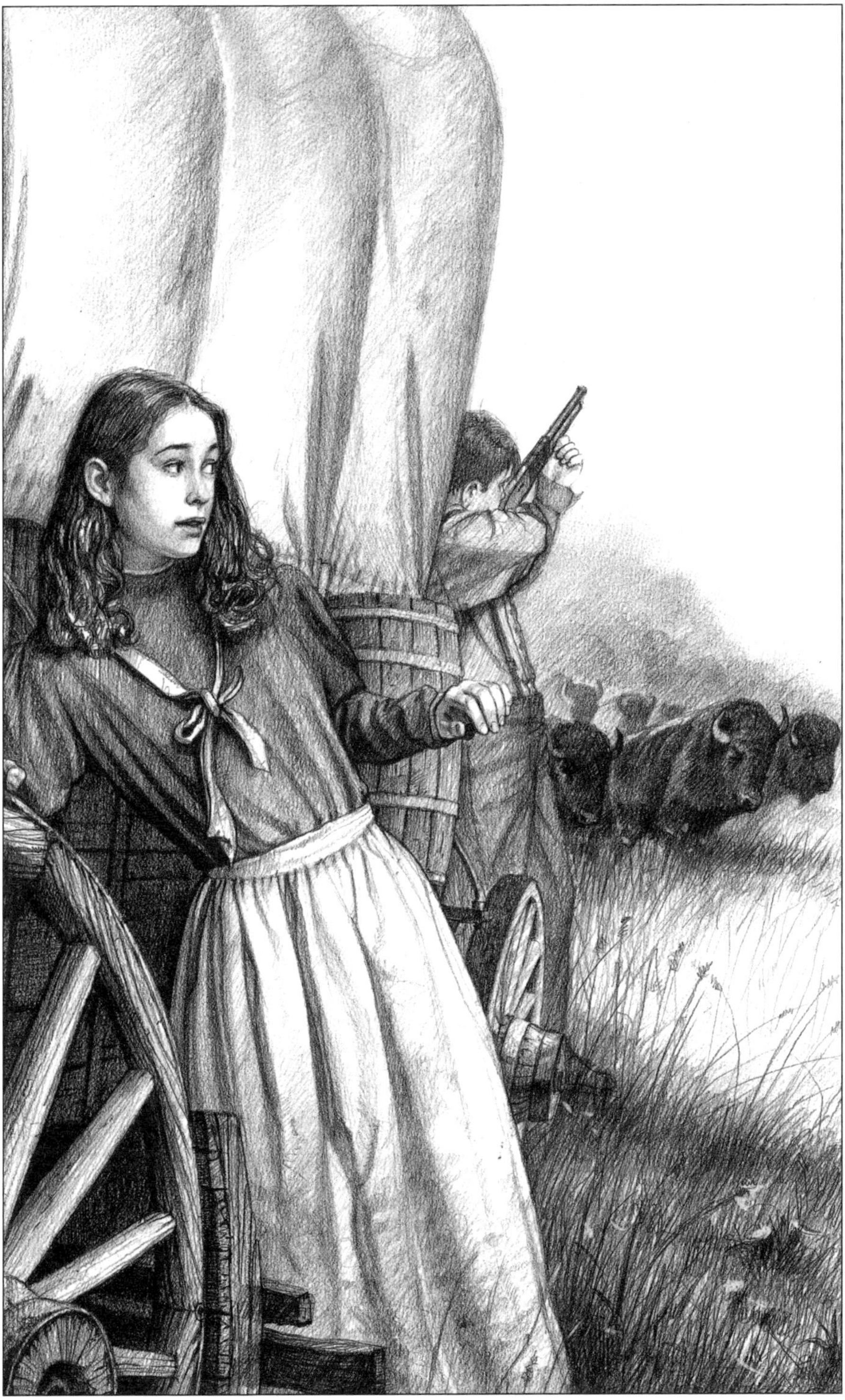

reloaded, fired and reloaded. The noise was deafening. The buffalo were so close Lucy could smell them.

The sound of the shots and the light of the fires caused the buffalo to veer away just before they reached the circled wagons. They turned and thundered by ten feet from the corral. The half hour that it took the herd to pass felt like hours to Lucy. Finally the last straggler stumbled past, and the buffalo disappeared into a cloud of dust once more. Lucy felt her stomach settle slowly. Dust still filled the air.

The men stopped firing and sent up a cheer. In the calm after the cheers stopped, Lucy looked toward the western sky, where the setting sun colored the sky a gold and orange. She breathed a sigh of relief.

Frank broke the brief silence. "I hope we don't see any more buffalo. I've seen enough," he said. Lucy hugged him and ruffled his red hair.

"Thank goodness you saw them in time," said Mr. Scott. "Good work, Frank." He looked over at Lucy and smiled. "You too, Lucy."

Seth clapped them both on the back. "Sharp eyes, the two of you."

Aaron just smiled as his eyes flickered over Lucy's face.

Some of the men found several buffalo that had been shot dead. They butchered them, skinned them, roasted the humps and ribs and had a feast for all. The colonel showed Lucy's mother how he had prepared the tongue. "It's the tastiest part of the animal. Let our young heroes have the first slices," he smiled at Lucy and Frank.

SIX

*J*UNE 22, 1860. WE CROSSED THE PLATTE *today on a bridge next to some log cabins. It cost $5 a wagon to go across. Father complained, but it's the fastest and safest way to get across. I'd rather cross the river on a bridge than wade or swim. From here, it is goodbye to the Platte. I'm rather sorry to see the last of it, even though it is muddy. We should come to the Sweetwater River in a few days. It is terribly hot right now. I haven't seen much of Seth and Aaron, as they are very busy. We can see the Rocky Mountains from here, like a blue smudge across the horizon. I've never seen mountains before, so I'm pretty excited. They look like clouds from this distance.*

June 26. We finally arrived at Independence Rock! We have come more than 800 miles from Independence. Halfway to California—well, almost, at any rate. We're on the Sweetwater River now and camped at the very base of the rock. It's about 200 feet high, half a mile long, and it looks like a huge turtle. Seth says there is a superstition that wagon trains must be at Independence Rock by the Fourth of July in order to get across the Sierra Nevada mountains before the snows start. From here the Rocky Mountains look like a huge fortress of rock and snow across the horizon. Since we've made good time, we've decided to have a spree. We'll celebrate Independence Day early and wear something red, white, or blue. I have my blue calico dress and a blue hair ribbon, although my calico is faded almost to gray. Independence Day at Independence Rock!

At noon the next day, the men fired their rifles into the sky to start the party. Mrs. Gray used the rest of her precious lemons to make lemonade for a few families, while Lucy organized running races for the children.

Dr. Gray brought out his fiddle to play for square dancing. Mrs. Gray danced with Colonel Alexander, and Mr. and Mrs. Scott joined them. Lucy stood, hoping Seth would ask her to dance. She felt a tap on her shoulder and whirled around. There he was!

"Hey Curly," Seth grinned. Lucy blushed and looked at the others dancing. Seth followed her gaze and smoothed his mustache. "Aaron and I don't dance," he said. "Never learned how. But do you want to come climb Independence Rock with us?" He held a small covered bucket of axle grease to paint on the rock.

"Sure," Lucy said, a little disappointed that he hadn't asked her to dance. Still, Independence Rock with Seth was better than no Seth at all. She followed him to where Aaron was waiting.

"Lucy! Lucy!" Frank and his friend John came running over. "Where are you going?"

Lucy was annoyed. "We're going to climb

Independence Rock."

"Can I come?" Frank begged.

"Sure," said Aaron.

"You better ask Father first," Lucy said. Frank was such a pain.

Frank ran to talk with Mr. Scott, who looked over at Lucy and nodded. Frank ran back with John. "Father says I can go. And he said you were supposed to ask, too, and you know how he doesn't like you going off by yourself," he lowered his voice to a stage whisper, "with boys."

Lucy turned red. Seth and Aaron looked amused. "Fine, let's go," she said grumpily.

But, when they passed out of sight of the wagons, she hitched her calico dress and petticoat above her knees and yelled. "Let's run to the rock! I bet I can beat you!"

"You're on," laughed Seth.

Lucy hadn't run like this since she was back on the farm in Missouri. She led for the first hundred yards, enjoying the feeling of the wind in her hair. The ten-year-olds fell back, panting. Seth and Aaron ran faster until they caught up with Lucy at the base of the rock. They all threw themselves on the ground, gasping for breath and laughing.

Seth looked at Lucy with respect. "Hey, Curly, you run faster than any girl I've ever seen. We had a hard time catching up with you. Of course," he teased, "I would have beat you if I hadn't been carrying this bucket." Aaron caught Lucy's eyes and smiled unguardedly.

When Frank and John caught up with them, they all started slowly up a steep trail on the side of Independence Rock. The granite wall was covered with hundreds of names painted onto or cut into the rock. "Here it is, Lucy," Aaron called, pointing at an inscription.

"Cyrus Scott, Missouri, July 1855," Lucy read. She touched the painted letters, suddenly feeling her eyes sting with tears. It was strange to see her uncle's name on this majestic rock so far from home. "Thank you, Aaron," she said softly. He smiled slowly.

"They call this the Great Register," he said, "because so many travelers have signed their names."

"Here's my name." Seth called. "Hey, Lucy, come see." She hurried over. "Here, I'll paint your name for you," he said, dipping a stick into the bucket of axle grease. After Seth finished a last flourish on her name, it didn't take long for them to climb to the top of the rock, where they stood and gazed out over the view.

"When you look out at these vast plains you realize why our trip takes so long," said Seth.

"It's so different from home," Lucy said. She stared at the ridge of snow-capped mountains to the west. "The Rocky Mountains are beautiful."

"Yeah," said Aaron. "When we get there, you'll see they're covered with trees. Look over there." He pointed to where the Sweetwater passed between two distant cliffs. "That's Devil's Gate. We'll see it closer tomorrow. It's magnificent but treacherous."

Lucy turned, looking for Frank and John. They

were on the far side of the rock, looking down. John lay on his stomach, sticking his head over the ledge, but Frank was standing. "I'm the king of the Mountain!" he shouted, jumping up and down.

"Be careful, Frank," Lucy called. Just then, Frank's foot slipped, and, to Lucy's horror, he tumbled over the edge.

"Frank!" Lucy shrieked, racing over to where he had been standing. Seth and Aaron were right behind her. Peering over the side, she saw her brother lying on a ledge about six feet below. He was whimpering, and his left leg was bent under him. "Frank! Frankie, are you all right?" she cried. "What's wrong with your leg?"

"I can't move it. It really hurts," gasped Frank.

"It must be broken," said Aaron. "We've got to get him back up right away." Lucy closed her eyes and tried to slow her thumping heart. "Thank goodness for the ledge," she whispered. "He could have been killed."

"I've got an idea," Aaron said. "Seth, you lie here beside the ledge and hold on to my arms. I'll walk backward down the wall to Frank. Lucy and John can hold on to your legs to keep you from slipping over. I'll lift Frank back up to you."

Lucy prayed silently as Seth held Aaron's arms. Aaron backed carefully down the cliff. "How are you, Frank?" he murmured, bending over the boy and gently straightening his leg. Frank cried out and then whimpered. "It'll be better soon," soothed Aaron. "I'm going to lift you up, but I need you to

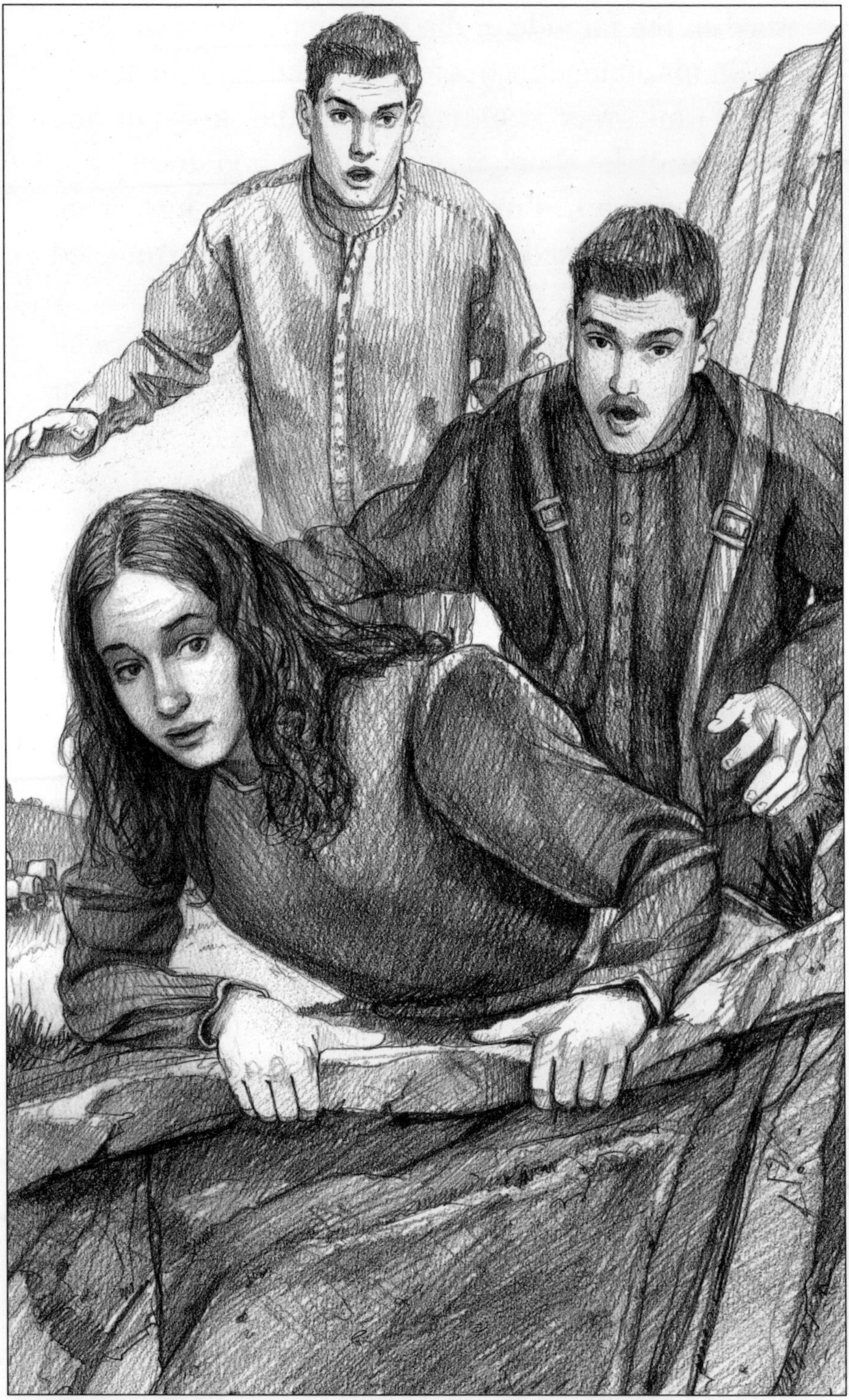

reach up to Seth. Can you do that?"

Frank nodded, white-lipped. Aaron lifted him to Seth, who grunted under the weight and dragged him over the edge. Seth laid Frank on the stony ground at the the rock's summit. Lucy hugged her brother, tears in her eyes. "Will you be all right until we get Aaron back up?" Frank nodded.

The three went back to the edge of the cliff. Seth gritted his teeth as he pulled on Aaron's arms. Aaron's feet scrabbled at the rock. Suddenly a rock gave way under his feet, and the ledge began to collapse. "Come on!" yelled Seth, pulling hard until Aaron was safely back on the rock. The boys flopped down, breathing hard. Lucy went back to her brother. The bone in Frank's leg stuck out at an angle, and there were tears in his eyes.

John, Aaron, and Seth came to her side. "I'll tear my petticoat so we can use the strips to hold the bone in place," said Lucy. The three boys turned their backs as Lucy reached under her dress and took off her dingy cotton petticoat. She tore it into strips, which Seth and Aaron tied around Frank's leg. When she handed Aaron one of the strips, she could feel his hand trembling. "Here, use my ribbon too," Lucy said, tugging the ribbon out of her dark curls.

"We're going to need help to get you down the rock, Frank," said Seth. "John and I will go back to the wagons. Lucy, you and Aaron stay with Frank. We should be back in half an hour." He and John began the hike back down the rock.

Lucy cradled Frank's head in her lap and sang

softly to him. Soon he was asleep. She and Aaron sat for a few minutes, saying nothing. Now that everyone else had gone, she felt nervous with him. She wished Aaron had gone for help and left Seth with her. Finally, her eyes drifted over to Aaron's face. "Who knows what would have happened to Frank if you and Seth hadn't been with us?"

Aaron looked into her eyes. "Don't worry about Frank, Lucy. He'll be fine. We—" Aaron's voice cracked, and he cleared his throat embarrassed, "Doc Gray'll know what to do." Aaron hesitated and then awkwardly patted her hand. His fingers slowly closed over hers.

Lucy looked up at him and blushed. She wondered if she should shake his hand off. What about Seth? But she liked the feel of his big, strong hand over hers. "Thank you," she said, trying to think of something else to say. "Do you—um—do you know any more Indian legends?"

Aaron's face brightened. "Lots. In fact, there's a legend about Devil's Gate. An evil spirit, who could change his shape to that of different animals, caused a lot of trouble for the Indians, so they hunted him down and shot all their arrows at him at the same time. He turned into a buffalo and then ran right through the side of the mountain. He was never seen again, but he left a big hole in the mountain where the Sweetwater passes through."

Lucy laughed. "I like that one." She paused. They were silent for a moment. "Why do you like Indians so much?" Lucy asked suddenly. "I've heard many stories of how they attack pioneers and massacre innocent people."

Aaron shrugged. "Well, that does happen sometimes, but I've also seen pioneers provoking them. One man on our last wagon train tried to cheat them at every trading post we came to. Some white folk have massacred Indians, too, or pushed them out of the way to make settlements. It's like a war, I guess."

"Am I right to be afraid?" asked Lucy.

"No. I mean—I guess it's not wrong to be afraid. Bad things have happened. But maybe sometimes it's the fear that makes it happen. I don't know—maybe that sounds stupid. I just wish you wouldn't be afraid." He looked at her and tightened his hold on her hand.

Lucy daringly squeezed back. "I'm learning a lot. I didn't want to come on this trip. But now—even though it's hot and dirty and—everything, I guess I'm glad."

"Good," Aaron smiled. "I love this land." Lucy smiled back and dropped her eyes. She couldn't believe she was sitting on top of Independence Rock holding hands with a boy. She liked Aaron a lot. She liked holding his hand. But what about Seth? She had thought she preferred him from the beginning.

They sat together until they heard Mr. Scott's voice calling. Aaron quickly dropped Lucy's hand. Seth, her father, and Dr. Gray soon climbed into sight. "We really broke up the celebration," said Seth. "All the men volunteered to come."

The doctor bent down and examined Frank's leg. "It's broken, all right," he said. Frank woke up and began to whimper softly again.

Mr. Scott patted his son's head as the doctor gently lifted him onto a piece of canvas they'd brought. "It'll be all right, Son." Mr. Scott reassured. "We'll get you down the rock and you'll be fine." But Lucy could see the worry in his eyes.

The men each took a corner of the canvas. Lucy led the way down the rocky trail. They were as gentle as they could be, but Frank groaned from time to time.

By bedtime the doctor had set Frank's leg properly. He gave him a small glass of whiskey to ease the pain, then tied a stake alongside the leg to hold the bone in place. "Go to sleep now, Frank," he said. "You'll be running again in a month or two." Frank groaned again.

Lucy looked at Frank's bandaged leg and wondered what had happened to her blue hair ribbon. It must have fallen off when the doctor set the leg. She looked around the tent but couldn't find it.

Lucy gave up the search and scribbled in her diary before she went to bed.

June 27. What a day! Frank broke his leg, I climbed Independence Rock, and Aaron held my hand. I am so confused. I know I like Seth best. He's fun, and I'm sure he likes me too. He wrote my name on the rock!

But Aaron is so nice. Holding his hand was wonderful. Father would be so angry if he found out. I think Aaron is sweet on me, and I like that. But I can't fancy two boys at once, can I? I don't know what to do. I wish I could tell Carrie. I miss talking with her. I MUST stop thinking about Aaron.

SEVEN

THE NEXT DAY, THE WAGON TRAIN STARTED out again, with Frank—cross and uncomfortable—lying inside the wagon. Lucy, now cooler without her petticoat, walked alongside, slapping at the swarming mosquitoes. The heat rising up from the dirt was awful. The trail crossed the shallow Sweetwater River several times as it ran through a steep canyon. The crystal-clear water of the river swelled the dried-out wood of the wagon wheels. Loose from crossing the dry bumpy plains, they were now snug in their metal rims again.

When they came closer to Devil's Gate, Lucy marveled at the sight of the water passing through the hole in the sheer cliff face. She thought of Aaron's story and looked up to find him riding by. "Isn't it magnificent, Lucy?" he asked eagerly.

"Yes," she said, nodding tiredly, thinking of Seth. She didn't know what else to say.

The pioneers were on their way through South Pass over the Rocky Mountains now. The ground sloped gently upward, covered with sagebrush. Lucy kept a sharp eye out for rattlesnakes as she walked; one man had been bitten a few days earlier and was very ill. As the wagons traveled higher into the mountains on the mild incline, they came to forests of aspen and pine. Fresh springs fed by melting fields of snow higher up, spilled into streams. Eagles nested on the tops of the lodge pole pines. The men hunted elk and deer to add fresh meat to the stew pot. When they stopped to make camp, Lucy picked purple columbine and bright red Indian paintbrush flowers. She placed some in her journal to press them.

July 5, 1860. We are at Pacific Springs now—the actual halfway point to California. It is the Continental Divide, about 900 miles from Independence. I had always imagined mounting huge slopes and descending into deep gorges when crossing the Rocky Mountains, but on the contrary, we have reached the very summit on a gentle, wide path, called the South Pass. The climb was unbelievably easy, though the air is thin here, and we lose our breath quickly. Our trail guide says we are 7,400 feet above sea level. The map shows that this is the first place the rivers run west as well as east. It is called Pacific Springs because the water from the springs runs down to the Pacific Ocean.

This morning, we woke up to find the buckets of water frozen over. I had to break the ice to fetch water for Mother. My chores have doubled since Frank's accident. He tends to sit back and pretend he's a little king demanding service. It's hard to feel sorry for him when he acts like that.

Sabrina has been very tired recently, and she rides in her wagon more now. I miss walking with her.

Seth has guard duty tonight. I hope he stops by. Aaron came over to talk the other evening, and I think I was rude to him. I feel horrible. I think a lot about our conversation on Independence Rock.

Lucy paused and stared into the fire. She wrapped her quilt closer. It was late; the big sky was dark and starry, the wind cold.

"Hey, Curly." She heard a familiar voice in the darkness. Seth put some more wood on the fire and squatted down next to her. "What's the matter? Can't you sleep?"

"Julia's crying because she's afraid of the timber wolves howling," she answered. "She woke me up, so I came out here to sit for a while."

"They don't scare you, do they?" teased Seth.

"No, I rather like their lonesome sound. As long as they don't come too close."

"Lonesome sound, huh? You're starting to sound like Aaron," he laughed. "Well, they won't come too near if we keep the fires burning. Wolves and coyotes don't like fire." Seth stared into the fire. Lucy wondered what he was thinking. She liked watching his profile against the fire, his mustache glowing faintly in the flickering light. She wondered what it would be like to sit before a fire with him in a cozy little house. She could sit in a rocking chair, knitting; he would sit like he was now, thinking . . . what?

"I guess I'd better get back on patrol," Seth said, standing up. "Good night, Curly." He tousled her hair and smiled.

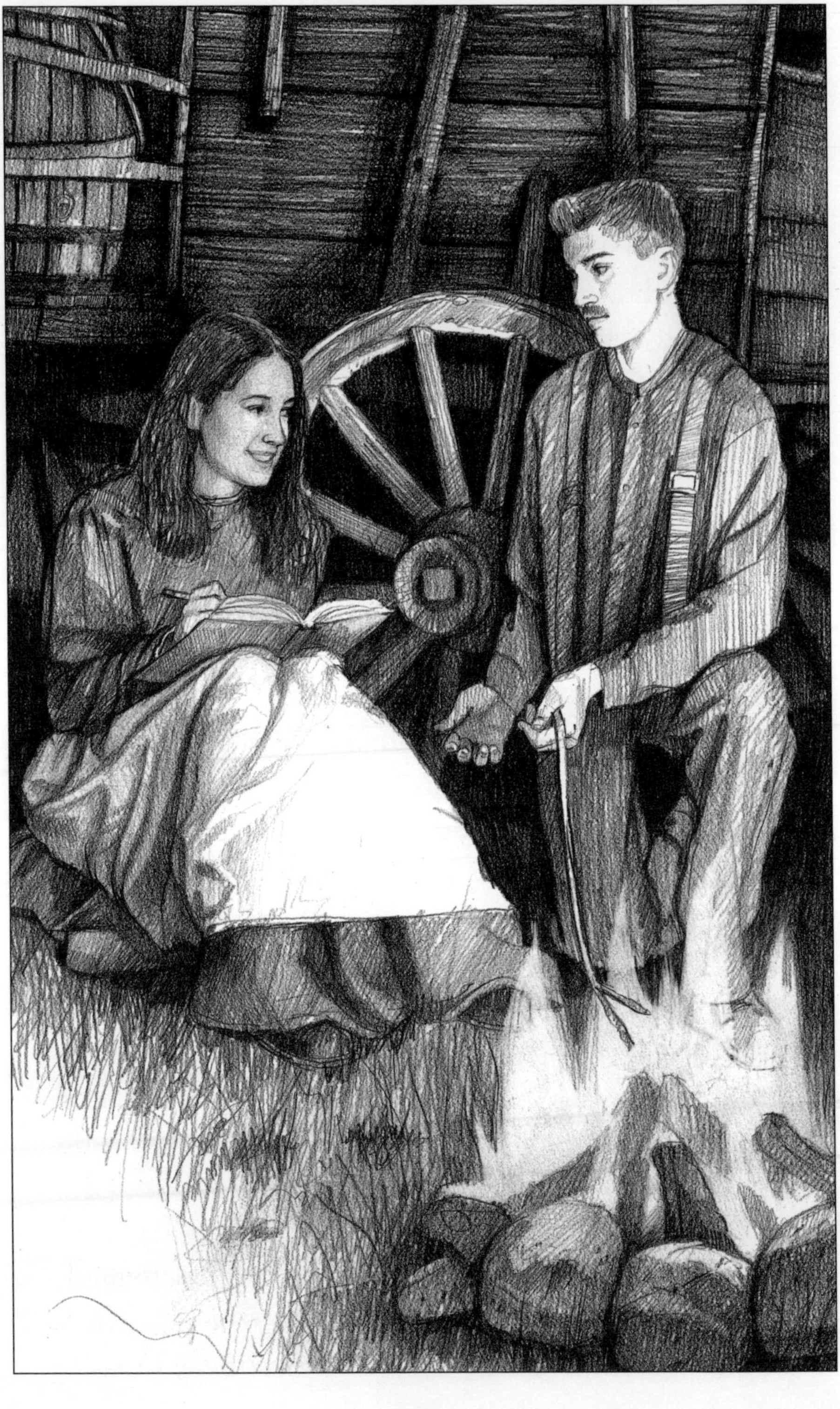

July 10. We are out of the Rockies now and have been traveling across dry, barren land covered with alkali holes. There's scarcely enough grass for the oxen and other livestock. We waited a day for the ferry over the Green River. The ferry was a big log raft that a man poled across the river. Seth told me that the Lombard Ferry, as it is known, is a stop on the Pony Express, so I finished up a letter to send to Carrie back in Missouri. But when I asked Father if we could send it, he said no. He said the Pony Express began this April, and they charge $5 just to carry one letter because they need so many riders and horses to make the trip between St. Joseph, Missouri and Sacramento, California. Riders can go for seventy-five miles at a time, but they change horses about every forty miles at relay stations along the way to keep them fresh. Anyway, Father said we'd just send the letter with a normal 10 cent stamp, and it will go by wagon or stagecoach. It will take twice as long that way, though.

I wish Seth would just tell me what he feels for me. It's frustrating to wait and wait and never really know.

July 14. We are at Fort Bridger now. The trail divides here. The Oregon Trail goes northwest, and the California Trail continues southwest. We met up with a wagon train bound for Oregon. The two groups of men are arguing about which is better—California, or Oregon—as a place to live. Of course, most of them have never been to either one!

Some of the women we met told Mother that several children in their train have died from measles. So horrible! Mother told us to stay away from the Oregon wagons.

Seth told me that Fort Bridger was a lot bigger when he first came through five years ago. He said it was originally a trading post established by a mountain man named Jim Bridger. The Mormons, who moved west so that they could practice their religion, took it over. Later the fort was destroyed during a dispute between the U.S. Army and the Mormons. Now the army is rebuilding it. Most of the houses here are log houses or made of canvas like our wagon tops.

Frank is hopping around on his leg now, though he still has to wear it in a splint. Sabrina and I waded in some of the streams here. Her feet are swollen, and she said it was a relief to soak them after so many long, dusty, hot days. I couldn't quite work up the courage to talk to her about Aaron and Seth.

There were some Shoshone Indians here trading when we arrived. They are tall and strong looking. Like the other Indians we've seen, they wear animal skins, beads, and feathers. I saw Aaron talking with them. He's been avoiding me again. Just as well. I'm afraid of making him think I fancy him.

A week and a half after leaving Fort Bridger, the wagon train passed through canyons and ravines. The trail passed near the Great Salt Lake, which Seth said was so buoyant that people floated on the surface when they went bathing in it. The salt in the ground sparkled in the desert sunlight. Colonel Alexander said they wouldn't go into Salt Lake City. They passed through wheat fields on the outskirts of the city that reminded Lucy of Missouri, although the wheat didn't grow nearly as high here. They passed a large, isolated homestead of Mormon settlers. Two women and several children came out on their porch to wave to the wagons. Around them, the Wasatch Mountains loomed gray and rocky.

August 7. We have been traveling through precipices and canyons—which is hard on the oxen, especially since there's not a lot of good grass along the way. Game is scarce along the trail now. The colonel says all the wagon trains are scaring them off. It is back to boiled beans and dried meat for us.

Now we are in the Thousand Springs valley. There are some amazing springs here—both hot and cold— although not many of them are good to drink. At least there's a lot of good grass. Another wagon train is camped here as well, and some of their children have the measles. I pray none of the children in our wagon train gets them. I think Julia is ahead of her level in reading now. If she is to be my only pupil, I must make certain to teach her well!

EIGHT

AUGUST 16, 1860. IT IS HOT AND DRY. NO trees or flowers to be seen—only snakes and other unpleasant creatures. If I never see another dry biscuit, I'll be happy. We're following the Humboldt River, but it's not good to drink, and there's not even enough grass for the livestock. We have to wade out and cut the grass that grows in the river for the oxen. There are no rocks or long grass for privacy when I relieve myself, so Mother, Sabrina, and I take turns holding our skirts in front of each other to keep from being seen. Poor Sabrina has to go a lot nowadays. She doesn't look very good. Many of our number are feeling ill from the heat.

Julia hasn't been attentive during our reading lessons lately. She gazes off into nowhere, and I keep reminding her to pay attention. It's not like her.

Before dawn the next morning, Lucy woke up to a whinnying sound. She sat up in her bedroll as she heard it again. Was it the wind or a coyote howling? She heard the noise again. A shadow galloped by. One of their horses.

Oh drat, Lucy thought. *No one else is awake.* She

didn't want to wake her parents; she knew they were exhausted. Instead, she stuck her feet into her heavy shoes and pulled her rumpled dress over her nightgown as she ran for their other horse. Untying him, she jumped astride his bare back. As she led him between the wagons and out of camp, Aaron woke up from under his quilt spread before the fire.

"Where are you going, Lucy?" he called softly.

"One of our horses has gotten loose, and I have to go get him," she called back.

It was very dark once she left the smoldering coals inside the wagon circle. The stars were shining, but there was no moon. Lucy stopped to allow her eyes to adjust to the darkness. Hearing the sound of hooves behind her, she turned and saw Aaron and Seth, ghostly white in the darkness behind her.

"We thought you could use a hand," said Seth.

"We'd better stay together," said Aaron, pulling his horse up next to Lucy. "Your horse probably bolted at the sound of the coyotes."

"We'll have to go slowly or our horses will stumble in the dark," said Seth. "But your runaway will slow down as soon as he's tired out."

They rode for a long time, and, when the sky started to lighten, Lucy saw her horse standing, halter dangling from his neck.

"I'll fetch him; he knows me," said Lucy. The horse seemed worn out, and Lucy had no trouble grabbing his rope and leading him back to the boys. The three riders and four horses walked slowly back to the wagons.

Breakfast was ready when they arrived back at

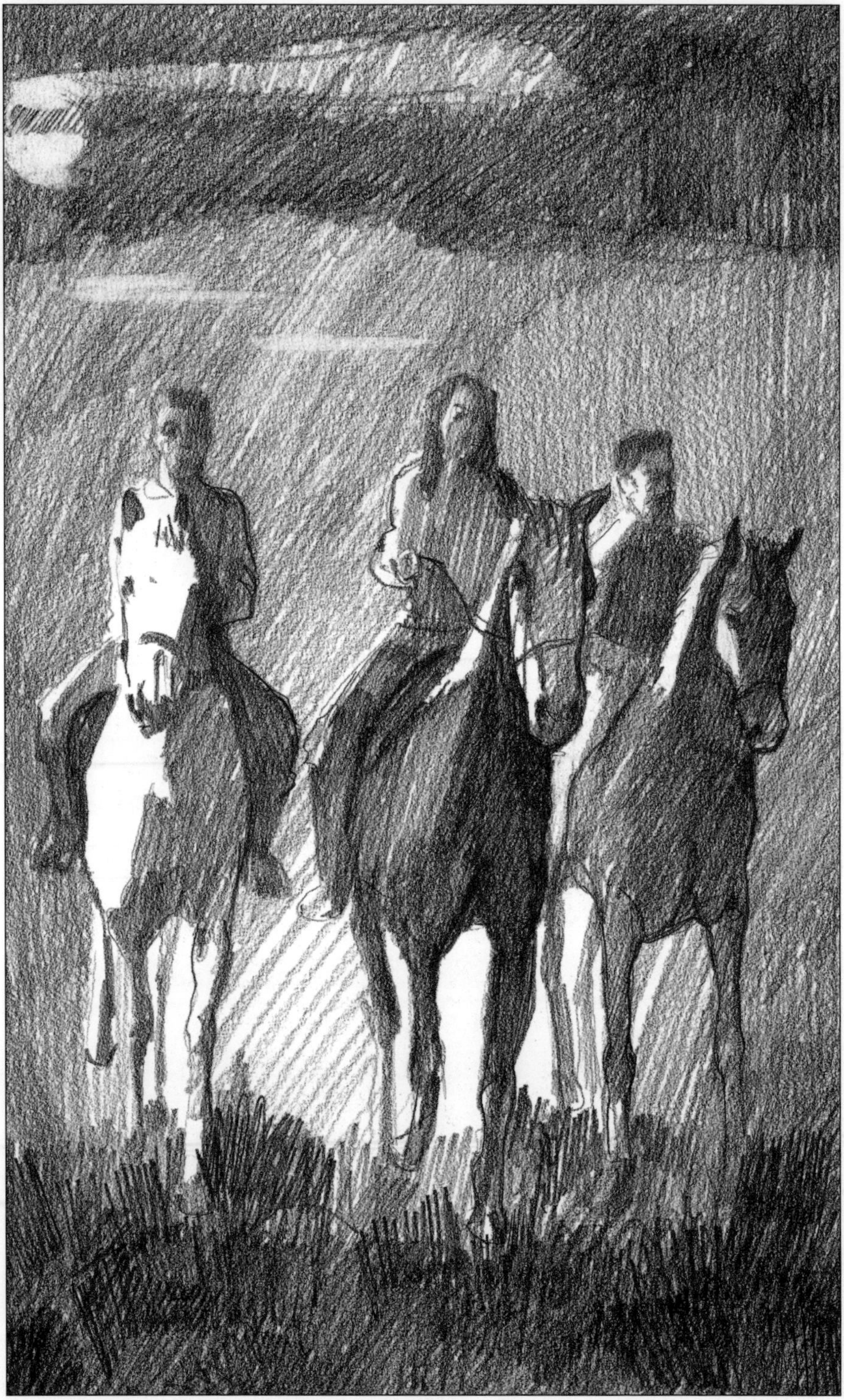

the camp. "Where have you been, Lucy?" Mrs. Scott asked anxiously as they rode up. Lucy's nightgown showed below her dress, her curls were jumbled, and she wasn't wearing her stockings.

Mr. Scott stood quickly when he saw them. He looked angry and worried.

"Lucy rescued your horse, sir," Seth said. "Aaron and I thought we could help her, but it ends up we were just along for the ride. If she hadn't heard him run away, you'd have lost him."

Mr. Scott smoothed his beard. "I didn't know the horses were gone. Well—thank you, boys. Next time, Lucy, wake me up. You did a fine thing bringing him back, but you could have gotten lost."

Lucy sighed with relief. Her father hadn't made a scene. She crawled into the wagon beside Frank for a nap. Julia came in and squeezed between them. They slept even as the wagon train resumed its westward journey.

*   *   *

That evening, as Lucy sat before the fire teaching Julia to read, her little sister flopped her head on her hand and stared listlessly at the page.

"What does this say, Julia? Sound out the words you don't know," Lucy prompted.

Julia looked away from the page. "I don't feel like reading. I have a headache." She coughed.

"You don't look so good, either. Even worse than usual," teased Frank. "Your neck's all swollen."

Lucy looked closer. Julia's throat did seem swollen. "Mother come look at Julia," she called.

Mrs. Scott pressed her lips to Julia's forehead, a look of worry on her face. "She's got a fever, and she looks like you two first did when you had measles back in Missouri. She must have caught it from the wagon train back at Thousand Springs." Mrs. Scott poured some of their precious drinking water on a clean rag, wrung it out, and put it on Julia's forehead. "We must keep you away from the other children. And no more reading until you are better."

The next morning, Lucy walked beside the wagon. Dust puffed up with each step. As she walked, she saw several graves. They were covered with piles of stones to keep the wild animals from digging up the bodies. Some of the graves had crudely-made markers with names on them. One said the child buried there had died from dysentery; another had fallen out of a wagon and was trampled. Lucy worried about Julia. Measles could be deadly, too.

She heard a horse behind her. Aaron rode up. "Recovered from your midnight ride yet?" he asked, smiling. Lucy looked at him surprised. His teasing sounded almost like Seth's.

"Yes," she smiled, glad he wasn't avoiding her anymore. "But Julia's sick now. I think it's measles." Her eyes strayed to one of the graves, sending a shiver down her back.

Aaron looked at her with sympathy. "I hope she makes a good recovery. But most everyone gets measles, and it's easier when they're young, anyway.

Seth and I had measles when we were nine."

"But you weren't on the trail then, were you?" asked Lucy.

Aaron bit his lip. "No, no. I reckon not."

*   *   *

The wagons continued, along the Humboldt River. A few days after Julia came down with the measles, just as she was breaking out in spots, some of the other children became ill. Mothers grimly traded ideas on how to keep the sick children comfortable in the heat and vainly tried to keep those still healthy away from the diseased. Nearly two weeks after Julia fell ill, they arrived at the Humboldt Sink, where the Humboldt River sank into the desert. Lucy crouched underneath the wagon—the only shady place she could find nearby—to write in her journal.

August 30. This trip is getting harder and harder. The worst of Julia's measles is over, but some of the other children in camp have worse cases than she has. Our animals are just as tired as we are. We are running out of feed for them, and there is no grass for them to eat. Yesterday one of the oxen from another wagon fell from exhaustion and had to be shot. It was butchered for meat, the carcass left by the side of the trail.

This is an awful place. We can see large volcanic hills rising out of the desert, and animal skeletons bleach in the sun. The ground is full of salt, and alkali dust blows through the air, burning my nose and throat. Even a damp handkerchief tied around my face doesn't help. The sand is deep and hard to walk in, and it scorches my feet. The water is hot and has a nauseating smell.

Seth doesn't stop by so much. He looks tired. Aaron and I haven't talked about the time we held hands on Independence Rock, but I'm much less awkward with him now. He's like a big brother to me. He says we have another forty miles of desert before we get to the Sierra Nevada mountains.

That afternoon, Colonel Alexander called the pioneers together for a meeting. Everyone was there except for the sick children and their mothers. "The next part of the desert is very harsh. It's hotter and drier than anything we've seen yet," Colonel Alexander told the group.

"How much worse can it get?" Lucy said to Sabrina. Sabrina clutched her stomach nervously and shook her head.

"There's a full moon tonight," Colonel Alexander continued. "It will take us all night and all day tomorrow traveling without water or grass to reach the Carson River. But there we can rest the animals a day before we start to the Nevada Mountains."

"Will there be enough light to see where we're going?" asked one man. "I don't want to break an axle."

"Even if there were no moonlight, we would probably be all right. The ground is flat," Aaron assured him.

Suddenly one of the women stumbled out of the wagons. "My Colin is gone," she wept. Her husband rushed over to her.

"What happened?" asked Mrs. Scott, as she went to the grieving woman.

"I thought he was getting over the measles," she sobbed. "But last night he seemed feverish, so I took a little of our water to give him a drink and to sponge his face. He went to sleep peacefully, but when I went to wake him, he was dead." The woman broke into wails.

Lucy stood where she was, stunned, while her mother put her arms around the woman. Nothing they could say would help her. She cried until her sobs subsided to gulps. Lucy shivered. Julia had played with the little boy only two weeks ago, and now Julia's scabs were peeling away, while Colin was dead.

Colonel Alexander took the father aside and quietly told him that they must bury the child as soon as possible. It was too hot to do otherwise. Aaron and Seth dug a hole. They wrapped the little body in a blanket, buried him, then said some prayers and sang a hymn with the group assembled at the grave. The pioneers settled down for a few hours of sleep. They would leave at two o'clock in the morning. Lucy stared up at the stars that seemed almost close enough to touch from where she lay. She felt tears seeping out of her eyes and into the ground. Everything—her worries about Aaron and Seth, her dreams of the future—seemed unimportant in the face of death. Lucy wished she were back in Missouri. She dreaded the crossing of the desert that night. She felt dust in her mouth, but she could not rinse it out. Water was too precious for that.

NINE

AT TWO O'CLOCK, THE WAGONS PRO-
ceeded by the light of the moon. The desert was
strewn with abandoned wagons and bones of oxen that
gleamed eerily in the moonlight. The abandoned
wagon beds were crumbling, and their tattered canvas
tops fluttered in the hot night breeze.

This trail has claimed so many lives, Lucy thought.

She heard the muffled tread of horse's hooves on
dust behind her. "Hey there, Curly," Seth said, dismounting. His hair seemed silver in the moonlight.
"I'll walk with you for a while."

Lucy turned to him. "I can't stop thinking about
little Colin."

Seth shook his head sadly and patted his mustache.
His horse walked silently beside him. "It's hard, yes. I
remember the first time we made this trip, six children
died. It's a rough trail." They walked along in silence.

Lucy turned to Seth with a sudden courage.
"Seth, I don't know what I would have done without
you on the trail. I always feel better with you around.
I hope—I hope I will—will continue to see you in
California." She stopped at the strange look on
Seth's face. "We will be close, won't we?"

Seth looked away and laughed lightly. "I couldn't say. Well, I'd best be off." He tipped his hat to her before mounting his horse and riding off.

Lucy watched him leave, confused. What was the matter? Had she said something wrong? Why had he rushed off? Her heart sank. She wished she could just lie down in the dust and sleep for a year or two and forget about everything.

September 1, 1860. We traveled by night, the rest of the day, and part of the evening until we reached the Carson River. Walking over this desert was like wading in dust. A two-inch long black scorpion stung one of the men, and Doc Gray was really worried for a while. The man didn't die, but he lay in his wagon as his wife took the reins. This desert is hard on Sabrina, too. She tried to walk a little during the night when it wasn't so hot, but it was too difficult and she got back in the wagon.

We are resting here today and tomorrow at the Carson River so that the animals will be strong enough to continue the journey. There are lovely cottonwood trees by the river and grass for the oxen to eat, also several outposts of traders selling things they have scavenged from abandoned wagons. They came out to meet us in the desert trying to sell drinking water. Father said it was a shame for people to charge money for water, but he bought some for the animals anyway. We were so exhausted and thirsty, that water, even if we had to pay for it, was definitely welcome.

Seth hasn't talked to me since the night after Colin died. But I shouldn't worry so much. There hasn't been time for any socializing.

The pioneers rested for two days at the Carson River, and then continued to journey on a well-established shortcut across another desert until they came to the Carson Valley three days later. But when they made camp in the wooded valley, Colonel Alexander warned everyone that the hardest part of the journey was still ahead. "We'll travel for another two days through the Carson Valley and then pass through a canyon into Hope Valley before we begin to climb the mountains. Although it is only about a hundred miles to Sacramento as the crow flies, the eastern slope of the Sierra is so steep that it makes moving the wagons slower and harder than any place we've passed through."

Lucy groaned. Colonel Alexander continued. "The weather is still warm, so we shouldn't have problems with snow going over the mountains, like the Donner Party had."

Lucy had heard her parents speak of the Donner Party, but never learned the full story. Aaron stood near her, so she tugged on his sleeve. "What was the Donner Party?" she asked.

"The Donner Party started over the mountains late in the fall of 1846," Aaron explained. "There was an early snowfall, which covered up the trail, and they had to camp near the top of the Sierra for the whole winter."

"Was it very cold?"

"Yeah." Aaron nodded. "It was freezing and

snowfall was unusually heavy that winter. Because they had planned to be in California before winter arrived, their food ran out. Some of them ate parts of those who died, to keep from starving. Many of them died before others succeeded in returning with help the following spring."

Lucy shuddered. "Too many pioneers die on this trail," she said.

Aaron stared up at the mountains, which rose almost perpendicular before them. "True," he said softly. Then he smiled and patted her on the shoulder. "But, we'll be all right. We're here in plenty of time to cross before winter. Remember, it doesn't help anything to be afraid."

September 7. Frank can walk without his crutch now. The measles scare is over, and Sabrina is feeling better as we begin to cross the mountains. We passed through a canyon at the end of Carson Valley today, and we are camped in Hope Valley tonight. It is the most beautiful little valley, with streams and pine trees.

The trail through the canyon was very rough. The tired, thin oxen had a hard time pulling the loaded wagons, and we haven't really even started to climb seriously yet. We had to lighten our loads today. Poor Mrs. Gray had to leave the last of her furniture, some beautiful cut-glass lamps, by the trail. Mother had to leave her rocking chair and Grandmother's china. I wonder what the next group of pioneers will think when they see all these things? At least, we're keeping

Grandfather's portrait! Seth is avoiding me. It hurts me. I wish I knew why.

The trail up the first slope of the Sierra Nevada was as steep as Colonel Alexander had said, and the going was hard. When the wagons came to a place where the trail was just wide enough for the people and animals to walk up single file, the wagons had to be pulled up empty. First the men drove the oxen and horses up the path while the women and children walked up behind them. Lucy had to help Sabrina who was afraid of heights and unsteady on her feet.

While the women, children, and animals waited in the cool pine forest, the men attached ropes and chains to each wagon, pulling them up the hill one at a time. Even though the distance was only about a quarter of a mile, it was slow, backbreaking work, with bleeding and rope-burned hands to show for it afterward.

They reached the first summit and camped in a little lake valley with pine forests and granite out-croppings rising around it. It was late afternoon, and the men were exhausted. But Lucy felt restless. She made her way over to Sabrina's wagon where the older girl was resting and asked her if she wanted to go for a walk. She'd finally decided she needed to talk to someone about Seth and Aaron. Maybe Sabrina could help her sort out her feelings.

The forest of pine and spruce trees seemed dark after the hot sunlit desert. Lucy didn't want to get lost again, so she marked the way with twig signs as Seth had taught her.

"Isn't it nice and cool?" she asked Sabrina. She wrapped her shawl tighter.

"It's nice to be surrounded with green for a change. I'll never forget that horrible desert," Sabrina answered as they walked over the pine needles, listening to the birds. They inhaled the aroma of incense cedar, rich and fragrant and walked without speaking while Lucy tried to think of a good way to introduce the topic of Seth and Aaron. Just as she was about to speak, Sabrina cried out. "Ohh—"

"Are you all right?" Lucy asked, concerned.

Sabrina clutched her stomach. "I have a terrible pain."

"Oh, no," Lucy said. "We'd better start back."

They turned around, but a few minutes later Sabrina cried out again. "I think the baby's coming!" she said anxiously.

"Oh dear," Lucy answered. "Let's hurry."

Sabrina gasped and sat down on a big rock. "Oh, it hurts. I don't think I can go any farther."

Lucy bit her lip. "Stay here. I'll run back for help."

"Oh, no," whimpered Sabrina. "Don't leave me alone. What will I do? There might be animals."

"But I don't know what to do! I'll go get my mother."

"Please, no," gasped Sabrina. "Don't leave me."

Lucy knew that pains this close together meant the baby was coming soon. "Take deep breaths. That's what the doctor told my mother when Julia was born."

Sabrina tried breathing deeply. She took two or

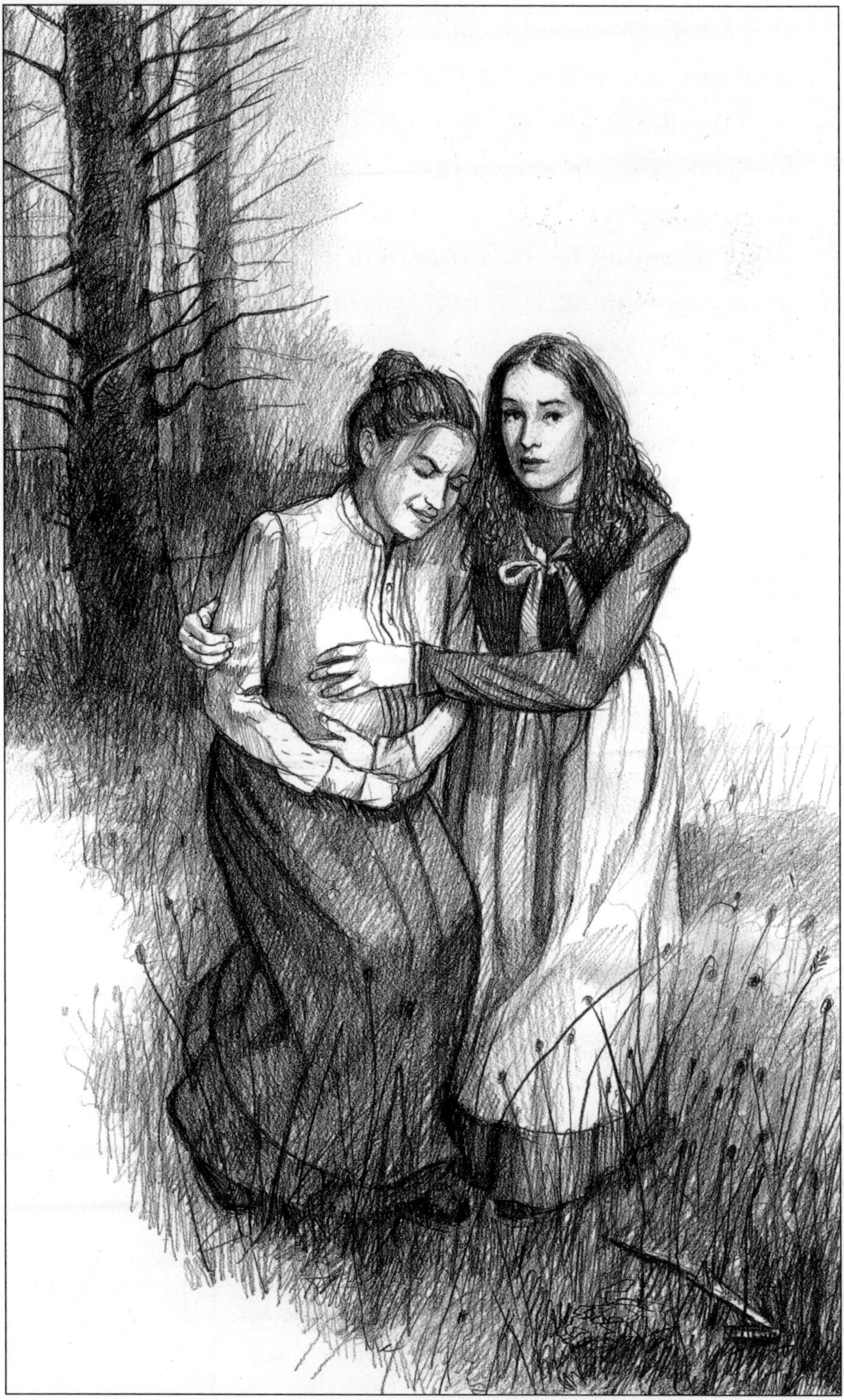

three breaths and let out a sharp cry. "It hurts," she wailed.

Lucy knew there was no time to lose. "We have to get you back to camp fast," she said. "I know you think you can't walk, but you have to. Here, I'll put my shawl around you, and you can lean on me." Sabrina whimpered as they slowly walked toward the wagons. The twig signs made it easy for them to find their way, stopping only for each of Sabrina's contractions. When they came into sight of the wagons, Lucy eased Sabrina to the ground and ran for her mother.

They succeeded in helping Sabrina into her wagon and finding Dr. Gray in time. While he was helping to deliver the baby, Lucy went to find Sabrina's husband, Tom. He hurried up as the new baby took his first cry. Climbing quickly into the wagon, he kissed the new mother. The doctor flashed Tom a warm smile as he handed him the little boy wrapped in a small, clean blanket. Tom gazed at the tiny baby. "Let's name him Charles after your father, Sabrina."

Sabrina smiled and nodded. Tom gently placed the baby in her arms and crawled out of the wagon. "Thank you so much, Lucy," he said, pumping her hand. "If Charles were a girl, we'd have named him after you!"

Lucy went back to her wagon, where her father looked up from cleaning his rifle. He smiled. "I heard all about it from your mother, Lucy. Good work. You are quite the heroine."

TEN

LATER THAT EVENING, LUCY SMILED AS she thought of Sabrina's baby. The whole camp had filed past to see the tiny bundle in his proud father's arms. Seth and Aaron sat before their camp-fire, talking. Lucy began to walk toward them, rehearsing what she would say to Seth. She would tell him how the twig signs had helped her quickly find her way back to camp. It was a perfect excuse to talk with him again.

"Hello, Lucy," smiled Aaron. "I hear you were the first to see the newest little pioneer."

Lucy smiled. "Actually, I came over because—"

"Yeah," Seth interrupted. "Such a tiny baby." He turned to Aaron. "When Emily and I have a baby, I reckon it'll be that little."

Lucy froze. Had she heard right? What did Seth mean? "Who's Emily?" she asked casually, forcing a smile.

Seth looked away. Aaron looked at Lucy and then Seth. "Emily? Emily is Seth's sweetheart. They're planning to get married when we get home. I figured Seth told you about her."

Lucy's smile felt like it was plastered on her face.

She couldn't believe her ears. Seth was planning to get married and he never told her? No wonder he acted so strange when she let him know how much she liked him. She felt the blood rush to her face.

Seth stared at the fire, looking embarrassed. "I guess I never mentioned her. I forget that people don't know about her. Yeah, we're getting married soon."

Lucy held her head high. "Well, congratulations. She must be nice." She knew her cheeks were red. She wanted to burst into tears and crawl under the wagon and never come out again. "Well I'd better be getting back to my wagon." She could feel tears coming to her eyes. She stumbled away as fast as dignity would permit. She hadn't even had a chance to tell Seth about the twig signs.

Back in the wagon she threw herself down, glad the rest of the family was away at least momentarily, and cried until her face was red and puffy. She pulled out her journal and cringed as she read everything she had written about Seth. Surely he had known she had feelings for him. Why hadn't he told her about Emily? He had stopped by so many times and made her think that he liked her specially. And what about Aaron? *Aaron must have known how much I liked Seth. What must he think of me? How will I ever be able to face him again?* Lucy wrapped herself in her quilt and cried herself to sleep.

When they awoke the next morning, the water in their bucket was frozen. Lucy put on all her clothes to keep warm. Her ragged dresses no longer touched the ground; she had grown taller, and they had shrunk. As the family ate a hurried breakfast, Mr. Scott stared at Lucy, who was huddled unhappily by the fire. "What's wrong, Lucy? You look like you just bit into a lemon."

Lucy refused to smile. Mrs. Scott looked at her worriedly. "I'm all right," she muttered and turned her face away. As they followed the trail toward the next mountain, Lucy walked alone. She didn't want to talk to anyone. She pretended that she didn't see Seth and Aaron when they rode by to check on the line of wagons. It was all so clear now. It was Aaron she liked—she'd liked him all along—not Seth, who had never felt the same about her. How could Seth have led her on like that? Or had he led her on? Had she deceived herself because she wanted him to care for her? If only she had found out about Emily months ago, how different everything would be. Now, she didn't think she could face either twin ever again. Aaron had surely seen that she cared for Seth. Oh, how humiliating.

I'm such an idiot. I'm such an idiot, Lucy repeated to herself. She wished she could just lie down and sleep until she forgot all about Seth. But she had to keep going. Step after step to California.

*   *   *

The climb to the second summit was not as strenuous as the climb the previous day. By late afternoon, they reached snow, which lay crisply on either side of the trail and up the rest of the mountain. Julia and Frank ran back and forth tossing snowballs. "The first snow this year!" Frank squealed. Lucy stared at the wildflowers that grew alongside the snow. Ordinarily, she would be delighted, but now she didn't care. She plodded alongside of the wagon to the summit of the mountain, eyes on the ground.

"Look, look, Lucy!" Julia called, tugging her away from the wagon. There before them was a vast view of wooded mountains, misty hills, and rippling streams stretching for miles and miles. A little further down the trail lay a mirrored lake reflecting a few retreating rain clouds and a fringe of pine trees, a rainbow shining over it all in the setting sun. It was beautiful. It was California.

Lucy couldn't help but feel her heart lightening. Finally, the trip was nearly over. "We'll be in Placerville in two more days and then on to Sacramento," she heard one man cry. Lucy felt the corners of her lips tugging upwards.

The wagon train cheered. Men tossed their hats in the air. Children clapped and danced alongside the trail. Women laughed. Even the animals walked faster as the wagons started down the mountain trail through the woods and foothills toward the Sacramento Valley.

*　　　*　　　*

Lucy turned at the sound of hooves. Seth looked down at her just as he always had, his mustached lip curving in a teasing grin. Lucy decided she didn't

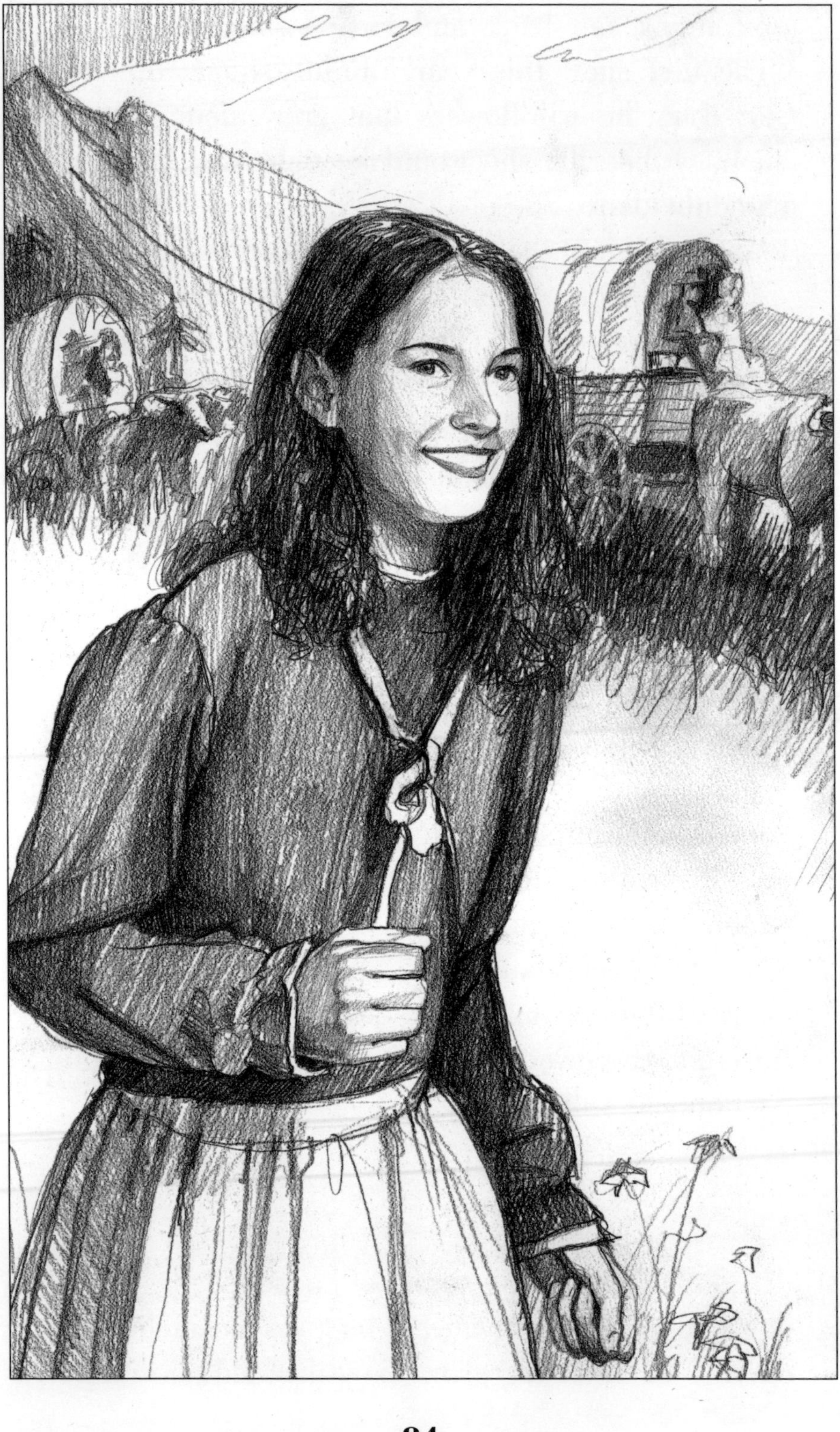

like mustaches after all. She stared at her wet shoes.

"We've made it to California, Curly. How do you feel about the trip now?"

Lucy tossed a dark curl over her shoulder. She also decided she didn't like being called Curly. "You were right, Seth," she managed icily. "It was an adventure in more ways than one. Excuse me."

She was going to tear up her journal. She walked back to their wagon, without watching where she was going. She marched headlong into someone. "Whoa," Aaron said, raising his hands and then settling them on her shoulders. Lucy looked up, red-faced. He was so close she could smell his buckskin. "I—" Aaron began. "I'm glad you were on this trip, Lucy," he said. He patted her shoulder awkwardly and turned to walk away.

Lucy couldn't think of anything to say. As she watched him leave, she noticed a little bit of blue ribbon hanging out of his pocket. Her hair ribbon! Had Aaron kept her hair ribbon ever since Independence Rock?

Lucy didn't tear up her journal. Instead she wrote: *Maybe there's hope yet. Oh, I hope. I hope. I hope. If I'm right, how happy I'll be—*

ELEVEN

AFTER TWO MORE DAYS OF TRAVELING down the wooded mountains, the pioneers arrived in Placerville, a mining town at the foot of the Sierra Nevada. Spirits had never been higher, and everyone was eager to reach Sacramento. The next afternoon, the Scotts finally arrived at the road leading to Uncle Cyrus's house. Wheat fields rose all around them, as in Missouri, but here the mountains towered in the distance. It was the twelfth of September. Their journey had taken exactly five months. They would leave the wagon train here while the rest of the families would go on to Sacramento before separating.

Lucy said goodbye to Mrs. Gray and then to Sabrina, who sat holding baby Charles on her wagon seat. "We've gone through so much together. It will seem strange not to see you every day," Lucy said.

"You'll have to come visit us when little Charlie gets bigger," Sabrina urged. "We won't be that far away. I don't know what would have happened if you hadn't been with me the evening he was born." She bent down and hugged Lucy. Lucy turned away teary-eyed.

Seth and Aaron rode over to say goodbye. Seth peered down from his horse. "Well, we've had some good times, Lucy. Maybe I'll see you sometime. Good luck."

"Good luck to you and Emily," Lucy mumbled. He reached down to shake her hand, and after a moment's hesitation, Lucy shook it limply. He rode away.

Aaron stayed. He dismounted and took off his hat. He stood on one foot and then the other. He looked up and took a breath. "May I write to you, Lucy?" he asked, flushing.

Lucy instantly became jubilant. "Oh, yes!" She smiled up into Aaron's eyes. They were bluer than Seth's were. "You know how much I like to write," she laughed. "You can be sure that I'll answer you."

Aaron hesitated, then turned to go. He turned back. "May I come back and see you sometime soon?" he asked.

Lucy looked at her father who was shaking hands with the doctor. She bit her lip and nodded. "I'd love to see you again."

Aaron's serious face broke into the biggest grin Lucy had ever seen. He looked at her for a long moment, glanced rapidly at her father, and then leaned down and kissed her quickly on the cheek before jumping on his horse and cantering away.

"I'll be waiting to hear from you," Lucy called happily after him.

He turned, still grinning, and waved.

Lucy looked over at her mother. She was watching Lucy and smiling.

*　　*　　*

Lucy walked the rest of the way to Uncle Cyrus's house with a grin as big as Aaron's. Frank danced alongside of her, chanting, "Lucy and Aaron. Lucy Alexan—" Lucy tackled Frank and smothered him with her arm.

"What's that all about?" Mr. Scott looked down from the wagon seat.

"Nothing, Father." She smiled sweetly as Frank squirmed.

The clapboard house sat in the middle of a big wheat field. Aunt Cora saw them coming and ran as fast as her plump legs could carry her. "Oh, I've been looking for you for days!" she cried. "I'm so glad you're here. Look at you, Lucy. You're a young woman." She hugged Lucy. Uncle Cyrus came running from the barn and enveloped his brother in a big bear hug. With their red beards, it was hard to tell them apart.

It had been five years since they had seen Uncle Cyrus and Aunt Cora. Julia tumbled out of the wagon. Tears came to Aunt Cora's eyes, "Is this Baby Julia?" She hugged Mrs. Scott. Lucy looked at the two women together. Her mother looked terribly thin compared to Aunt Cora. Maybe that's the way they all looked now.

Lucy gazed across the golden brown valley at the coastal range to the west. A hot south wind was blowing, and the grass was dry and yellow. "It's hard to believe we're in California," she said. "The fields remind me of Missouri, but I thought it would be green here."

"It will be in the winter and the spring," Uncle Cyrus said, settling an arm on her shoulder. "But come on in and eat now. Cora was just calling me to dinner when you arrived."

"How wonderful to sit in a chair again," said Lucy, once they were settled at the table.

"And to eat at a table," said Mrs. Scott.

Aunt Cora fed them fried chicken, fresh carrots, potatoes from the root cellar, and an apple pie. They all ate more than they had in weeks.

"I like having real food," said Frank with a full mouth.

"I'll never eat dried beef or crackers again," said Lucy.

"I still feel like I'm in a wagon," said Julia. "I'm rocking." Everyone laughed.

"Fresh food is what I missed," said Mrs. Scott. "Look at the size of these carrots. Does everything grow so big here?"

"It's wonderful farmland," replied Uncle Cyrus. "The ground is fertile, and the weather is mild. You'll see. You'll be glad you came. There's plenty of room for you to farm with us."

Aunt Cora had made new linsey-woolsey dresses for Lucy and Julia. Lucy was pleased. She had worn her calico dresses every day on the trail, and they were dirty and ragged.

"I'd like to take these old dresses and burn

them," Lucy said to Julia. The new dresses were pretty and clean, but Lucy's was too short and Julia's too small.

"You've grown a lot in the five months since your mother's last letter," said Aunt Cora. "I'll have to let out the seams so they will fit."

Mr. Scott looked at Lucy. "You wanted to be a teacher when we left Missouri. Do you still?" Lucy nodded. "Cyrus says the farmers here in Wheatland are building a one-room schoolhouse, and they need a teacher," her father continued. "Cyrus, Lucy will be as good as any teacher you can find. She taught Julia to read on the trip out."

Lucy's mouth opened in surprise. She had been so busy thinking about Aaron that she hadn't thought about teaching.

"I don't understand," she said. "Why will you let me be a teacher here, when you wouldn't in Missouri?"

"There are two reasons, Lucy," said Mr. Scott. "First, you grew up on our trip west. When we left, you were a girl. Now you are a young woman. It's not just that you will be turning fifteen next month. You handled several emergencies well. I'm sure any situation you might meet as a teacher won't be nearly as challenging as rescuing Frank from a cliff, finding a lost horse, or helping to birth a baby. Secondly, teaching here, you'll get to stay with us. You are an important part of our family. We'd all miss you if you were in Missouri."

Lucy hugged her father. Sometimes he didn't act

like he cared about her, but he really did. "Yes, Father, I do want to teach here. That is just what I want to do."

Lucy sighed happily and walked over to the door, gazing out at the sun setting over the fields. She could see the next few years rolling out in front of her like the trail across the prairie. Now she knew the end. She would teach. Aaron would return. California was going to be wonderful, after all.

SELECTED BIBLIOGRAPHY

- Comfort, Gene and Betty. *The Trail to Oregon*. Dundee, Ore.: Vistas Unlimited, 1989. Video.
- Dary, David. *Seeking Pleasure in the Old West*. New York: Alfred A. Knopf, 1995.
- Friends of the Bancroft Library. *The Ralston-Fry Wedding, 1858*. Berkeley: University of California Press, 1961.
- Gregory, Kristiana. *Across the Wide and Lonesome Prairie, Oregon Trail Diary of Hattie Campbell, 1847*. New York: Scholastic, 1997.
- Guthrie Jr., A.B. *The Way West*. New York: William Sloane Associates, 1949.
- Harvey, Brett. *Cassie's Journey, Going West in the 1860s*. New York: Holiday House, 1987.
- Holling, C. *Tree in the Trail*. Boston: Library Classics, 1942.
- Levy, JoAnn. *They Saw the Elephant: Women in the California Gold Rush*. Norman, Okla.: University of Oklahoma Press, 1992.
- Myres, Sandra L. *Westering Women and the Frontier Experience 1800–1915*. Albuquerque, NM: University of New Mexico Press, 1982.
- Schlissel, Lillian, Byrd Gibbens, and Elizabeth Hampsten. *Far from Home, Families of the Westward Journey*. New York: Schocken Books, 1989.
- Schlissel, Lillian. *Women's Diaries of the Westward Journey*. New York: Schocken Books, 1982.
- Smithsonian Institution. *1846, Portrait of a Nation*. Washington, D.C.: National Portrait Gallery, Smithsonian Institution, 1996.